$1,50

TRINI
LIBRA

This book may be kept
FOURTEEN DAYS

fine will be charged for each
the book is kept overti

Go, Phillips, Go!

Other books by the author —

*WHERE WAS EVERYONE WHEN
 SABRINA SCREAMED?
*THREE LOVES HAS SANDY
 PLAY BALL, McGILL
 TO CATCH A SPY
 THE SPY WHO TALKED TOO MUCH

*Available from Scholastic Book Services

T A B
F I C
W 14 g

Go, Phillips, Go!

Amelia Walden

TRINIDAD HIGH SCHOOL

TRINIDAD HIGH SCHOOL
LIBRARY

SCHOLASTIC BOOK SERVICES
New York Toronto London Auckland Sydney Tokyo

3138

This book is sold subject to the condition that it shall not be resold, lent, or otherwise circulated in any binding or cover other than that in which it is published—unless prior written permission has been obtained from the publisher—and without a similar condition, including this condition, being imposed on the subsequent purchaser.

Copyright © 1974 by Amelia Walden. This edition is published by Scholastic Book Services, a division of Scholastic Magazines, Inc., by arrangements with The Westminster Press.

13 12 11 10 9 8 7 6 5 4 3 2   8 9/7 0 1 2 3/8

Printed in U.S.A.

01

ACKNOWLEDGMENTS

With grateful acknowledgment to Virginia E. Parker, instructor of physical education at Staples High School, Westport, Connecticut, for our discussions about the constantly changing game of girls' basketball and especially for her long-time valued friendship.

And to my brother, Bill Walden, who began his distinguished newspaper career as a sports reporter and covered many a basketball tournament.

CHAPTER ONE

Pete Phillips was the last one to run up the stairs from the locker rooms for basketball practice that afternoon. From the sounds in the gym, she knew that a game between the varsity and the junior varsity was already in progress. She heard the whistle blow, the booming of a man's voice issuing commands about charging and hacking. When she opened the door and stepped inside, she saw Camilla Gomez bouncing the ball at the free-throw line. Pete waited for Camilla to sink it in, then started for the bench where a few substitutes and some of the jayvees were spread out. She didn't get halfway there.

"Just a minute, Phillips." She stopped and turned. Burt Johnson, the new student-assistant coach, stood facing her. She had not been this close to him since that day two summers ago when he had caught up with her down in Bamberger Village. "Why, you've grown up, Pete," he had said. "No more dirty-faced kid with stringy hair!" There had been some changes in Burt since then. His hair was clipped shorter, the band across his forehead was gone. There was a different expression in his eyes, less of the mocking challenge. His clothes were more conservative — flannel trousers, a jersey top. But one thing had not changed, that air of smoldering excitement.

She thought he was going to bawl her out for

being late. Instead, he ignored her tardiness and said, "Phillips, play pivot on the varsity. You there, the girl in the green sweater, you come out. Get moving, Phillips, that's your spot. Go take it."

Whew, she thought, what a guy! He can't have been here more than half an hour and he's throwing his weight around like he was Red Auerbach bossing the Celtics. No wonder her seven brothers had resented him when they were playing in school.

She was thinking other things. Why, for instance, had he put her into the pivot spot? She had a long record as Central High's top-scoring forward. Even in practice games she had never been relegated to the position of pivot player. In college or pro basketball a pivot man could be responsible for much more than routine passing. But in girls' basketball, when you said, "Play pivot," you meant that someone was being sent in there to sprint and get the ball on a pass from one teammate and hurl it fast and accurately to the girl who would do the shooting. Pete thought, I won't even have to know where the hoop is, no less aim at it!

For ten minutes Pete played pivot to her teammates Connie Anderson, Bretta Masi, Jinnie Lawson, Tammy Kovaks, Camilla Gomez, and Angie Alvieri. Burt Johnson kept blowing the whistle on Pete's passes, criticizing them.

"That was a clumsy pass you just made," he would bawl. "Can't you do better?" Or, "You're handling that ball like it was a basket of eggs." Once he shouted, "Phillips, what are you afraid of?"

2

"I'm not afraid of anything. I'm just not cut out to play pivot. You're asking me and I'm telling. It's not my thing."

"What is your thing?"

"I make baskets."

"You make baskets, do you? Okay, we'll make a switch. You there, the girl in the blue shirt, change with Phillips. Go on in, Phillips, and show us how good you are at shooting."

It proved to be the worst half hour Pete had ever put through in the old gym of Central High. She tried to shoot. She honestly tried. But every time the ball hit her fingers, and she took aim at the hoop, that funny twist developed in her right wrist. She tried every shot in her bag — hook, lay-up, tip-in, bucket, jumper, pivot shot, a long lazy overhead. She even tried an easy bank shot and a shoulder heave-ho. She completed about one out of five or six tries. That was not only unspectacular, it was humiliating.

When Burt Johnson blew the whistle that ended the ordeal, she wanted to scream with relief. He motioned the girls to arrange themselves in a circle on the floor, and he sat, cross-legged, in the center of the group. In terse sentences he ran through every girl's game, summing up her weaknesses. He carried off this analysis with startling accuracy. His manner was impersonal and he kept his voice low-pitched. He would point out the mistake, then specify the way to correct it. Pete was glad to notice that he had stopped referring to them as "the girl in the green sweater" or "the girl in the blue shirt." His method was to ask each girl to state her last name. Then he made sure to use it.

"Alvieri, your passes are too high. You're over-reaching. You're tall enough to keep them lower. If you do, you'll get a much more accurate aim, so the girl running to catch the ball will have an easier reach ... Masi, you talk too much. Running off at the mouth interferes with your concentration. I've got nothing against 'mouthing' an opponent when you are trying to psych the other team out of its groove, but you overdo it. Hold your verbal barrage, then when you do use it, it will prove more effective. Basketball isn't a mouthy game. Talk less and keep your mind on the girl near the basket ... Anderson, you're short but you've got plenty of speed, a good eye, and a real clutch for the rebounds. But you're much too eager. You're working three times as hard as you need to. You can afford to relax because you've got speed to spare. Take it easy. Don't wear yourself out in the first quarter ... Kovacks, you've got one good shot. Your jump shot. That limits you. You need to practice other kinds. Have you got a basket in your backyard? Sure, you have. So practice a lot with that hoop. You've got a lot working for you. You're a big girl, with strong arms and legs. You should be good for a lot of other shots ... Gomez, you're plain lazy. You're playing like this was a dance marathon and it didn't matter what you did so long as you stayed on your feet. You need to stir your stumps and *move*. Move, Gomez. Practice sprinting or jogging. Get some of your friends to practice passing, dribbling, shooting with you. Someone like Anderson who has enough speed for herself and half a dozen others ... Lawson, you're not aggressive enough.

You need to build up the strong defensive tactics that make for a good offense. You're a pushover for a strong opponent who can psych you into backing off. Get someone aggressive to practice with you, like Kovacks, for instance, who can break your namby-pamby attitude. Basketball is a competitive game, Lawson — girls or no girls, you're in it to win. Every game is for winning or it's not worth playing. You're out to win, Lawson, not to dance a ballet."

Pete sat there, goggle-eyed, waiting for her turn. It never came. Burt went on through the second string and the junior varsity, giving each girl a few pointers for self-improvement. The name Phillips never came up.

"Okay, that's all for today," he said, glancing up at the clock. "We'll practice every afternoon this week. Friday night we play Southport at Southport. A night game is important, and it's essential that we practice heavily for it. The boys will be using this gym on Wednesday and Thursday. So I've asked if we can use Bamberger Hall. They said we could. Most of you live in the Village, so it ought to be convenient."

Bamberger Village was a section of Bradford often called Hamburger Heaven, or The Bum Burg. It was sometimes referred to as Bradford's ghetto. It's architecture ranged from big old places like Pete's home to the brick tenements, a housing project made possible by the financial support of Michael Bamberger, who had given the Village its name. And Michael Bamberger himself had also built an ugly brick gym and given it his name. So Burt's announcement met with suppressed groans.

"I admit it's not ideal, but it's the best I could do. All the other halls and gyms in the Village are in use. So show up. Don't miss practice. It's absolutely essential that we get the bugs out of your team play before Friday. That Southport game isn't going to be an easy one. You'll be on foreign soil, for one thing. Playing at home sometimes gives you more of an edge. Also, it's your first night game of this season, and the Southport fans are enthusiastic, noisy, often hostile. You'll have that to cope with. So give yourselves a break. Take advantage of the daily practices that I'm offering you." He nodded, dismissing them.

Pete started out of the gym. "Phillips, I want to talk to you."

He walked around, scooping up balls and stuffing them into bags. He let her stand there until they were the only ones left in the gym. He swung around and bounced a ball at her so swiftly that it startled her. She jumped back but caught it. Just about!

"Go ahead, star shooter, let me see you shoot."

"You saw me trying to shoot for half an hour and missing most of them."

"Don't tell me what I saw. Do what I tell you to do. Shoot."

She let go a long shot from where she stood. It missed. He bounced her the ball again. She ran toward the basket this time, took a spring and a leap and tried to land a jumper. It missed too. She got the rebound and fell back, deep into center court, and hurled the ball again. It missed. She caught the ball Burt tossed to her and ran up near the "keyhole" to try for a lay-up. It missed.

Out of about fifty tries, she sank maybe six or seven. And those six or seven were not the clean, neat shots to which she was accustomed. At last he called a halt. He looked at her for an uncomfortably long time before speaking.

"What's your real problem?" he asked.

"I'm not getting them through the hoop."

"Any clown can see that. I don't mean what's wrong with your game. That's the *effect*. What I'm after is the *cause*. What's fouling up your game? What's bothering you?"

"Nothing."

"Have you had your eyes examined recently?"

"Two weeks ago. They're perfect."

"Have any accidents that injured your arms or hands?"

"No."

"When did the problem with your shooting start?"

"I noticed it when I was practicing late in the fall. At first I didn't pay much attention. I'd just miss a basket and think, Oh, wow! That was a bum shot. Then it was happening too often to be just the misses you make no matter how good are you. So I decided I needed to practice alone and find out what was wrong. I switched to the town courts — nobody goes there much in winter. For a while I thought the trouble was clearing up. My shooting seemed to be more consistent. Then we played the Bradford High team last Friday and . . ." she stopped.

"What happened in that game?"

"My shooting wasn't bad, not real flaky like today, anyway. I had some tough competition, too. Bradford's got a new girl, a heavy shooter named Susan Alpert. I missed a few more than usual, but my game was pretty good on the whole. Yet there was this twist in my right wrist every so often. I couldn't control my hand and aim where I wanted to. What worried me was that I missed some easy shots, crip shots, short ones close to the basket that could have been made without interference. We won the game and I made the final shot, the winning one from center court. But it was a long chance I was taking and I knew it. I had missed those other shots because of whatever was wrong with my wrist."

He shook his head. "Negative. You didn't miss any shots in the Bradford game, or this afternoon for that matter, because of your wrist. You missed because you were upset by something either outside or inside yourself, and whatever was upsetting you threw your wrist too. In the Bradford game you were in control enough of the time to score high and you had sufficient command in those tense last few seconds to sink a shot when all the pressure was on you. If there was anything physically wrong with your wrist, that's when it would have shown up — but good. You were concerned, but you didn't chicken out. You stopped thinking about your hand and made the point. So I have a theory."

"What is it?"

"Somewhere, somehow, you've got your emotions involved in your game of basketball."

"Emotions! On the basketball court I'm steady as a rock. No temperament, never fly off the handle. I keep my feelings under control. And I do mean control!"

"Maybe that's your real problem."

"I don't know what you're talking about."

"The most dangerous people often are perfectly controlled people."

"How do you mean — dangerous?"

"To themselves. Everyone gets angry, sees red, wants to lash out and hit someone or something once in a while. So they kick a chair or hurl something across the room. Or pick a fight with the handiest guy. But not you. I needled you half a dozen times this afternoon, but instead of letting off the steam, shooting off your mouth, or hurling the ball at me, you stuffed the feelings inside and kept missing the shots."

"That sounds more like parlor-game psychoanalysis than competent basketball coaching." She kept her voice low-pitched. Going over to the bench, she picked up her sweat shirt. Without looking at him or asking if he was finished, she walked toward the door of the gym.

"Phillips!" She stopped but kept her back toward him. "Turn around." She did so, slowly. "I like people to look at me when I'm talking to them."

"I'm looking."

"You don't like me, do you?"

"I've never really thought about it. But I'll think real hard and let you know as soon as I make up my mind." She had the satisfaction of seeing a deep flush show through the reddish-bronze complexion of this strange, disturbing man. "May I be excused now?" she asked.

"Yes, Petrina, you may." She winced at the sound of her real name as he turned his back and walked away.

CHAPTER TWO

When Pete ran out into the school parking lot, a gust of raw wind almost blew her down. It had turned bitter cold. She looked for Connie and Bill, thinking they might have waited for her, but there was no sight of the battered station wagon in which Bill banged around.

Pete started across the lot, thinking it would be a blustery hike home, when a car pulled up beside her.

Recognizing the blue sedan, she called, "Hi, Shawn Patrick. I hope it's me you're waiting for tonight!"

"Who else?"

She had practiced with Shawn at the public courts. Not a hoopster, but a natural athlete with leadership and charisma, he had been drafted to boost the morale of the rival Bradford team.

As she climbed in she asked, "To what do I owe the honor?"

"The ill wind that blows some good. I got out of our practice early and almost got blasted into outer space. So, says I to myself, this is no night for a gal to be walking home from school."

"How did you know I'd be walking?"

"Gramp O'Hara."

"Gramp!"

"Yup. I drove down to your house and no one was home but Gramp. So I introduced myself

10

and said I was looking for you and did he know where you might be, and he said yessir, he sure did know. You'd be whacking a ball around at school, and you didn't have a car because your brother Paul had come and taken it back, and you'd probably have to walk home unless you got a ride . . ."

"You introduced yourself to Gramp. Now that's mean. I wanted to bring you to him properly and make a real nice introduction, very correct — boy meets girl and girl brings boy home."

She could see the corners of his mouth twitch as he answered. "Gramp seemed to know all about me. He said I must be the boy you keep talking about —"

"I don't keep talking about anyone! Gramp would never say that. He'd never —" She cut herself short, realizing that she had stepped right into the trap that Shawn had set for her. "You're teasing."

"Am I? Maybe it's just wishful thinking. Anyway, I've met Gramp, and he's everything you say he is. He's great."

"That he is." Gramp lived in his own little cottage in back of the big ancient house that sheltered his daughter's big family.

"Where do you want to go?" Shawn asked.

"Home, where else?" Home was a warm, happy, busy refuge.

"Lots of where elses. There are plenty of restaurants and diners in Bradford and environs. Personally I like a diner for a first date. You can talk and not be heard because of the jukebox and the clatter. It's cozy."

"I have a better idea. Let's barge in on Gramp

11

and have supper there. Then I can introduce you properly."

"Won't he mind?"

"Not Gramp. He'll love it. There's always plenty in his frig and even if he's eaten already, he'll be glad to watch us and sit and talk. Mom has a lodge meeting tonight, so no one will be home in the big house."

"Okay, if you say it's all right. Gramp must be quite a guy."

"Yes, he is," Pete agreed. She thought about Gramp. He was a quiet, bookish man. A man who liked people when he chose to be with them but who also enjoyed being alone. A man who liked to walk, in sunshine and rain. A man who sauntered down to the waterfront and fed the gulls and looked wistfully out to sea. A man who could talk enormously about any subject you brought up. A parlor Don Quixote, a romantic with a heart as big as all outdoors. A man who spoke what was on his mind, yet still a man with a secret. Gramp and Shawn took to each other like the proverbial duck to water. Pete warmed up some cannelloni that her mother had sent over, and she set places for Shawn and herself in the kitchen.

With an extra place mat poised in the air, she turned to Gramp. "You having a snack with us?"

"Just coffee. Later, when you bring out the pie, you can cut an extra piece for me. It's your favorite — homemade chocolate cream."

Pete could always tell when Gramp liked someone — really and truly liked — because he *talked*. And tonight he was in top form. He discussed all the topics that interested him — politics, books, sports, world affairs, the international situation. And celebrities, especially celebrities.

"Gramp's a regular gossip with the name-dropping," Pete explained to Shawn. "He garners all kinds of obscure information — never malicious, mind you — about important people. How he does it and where he gets his facts, no one will ever know."

"I read biographies," Gramp admitted.

"It sure enough isn't the kind of stuff you hear over the TV."

Then Gramp turned to Shawn. "Pete tells me you haven't any family relations to speak of, that you've been forced out on your own, at schools and such."

"That's right. My parents have never been anchored long enough in one place to make a home for us."

"No family life," Gramp shook his head. "That must be pretty bleak."

"I do have a kind of family life this year. Maybe Pete told you."

"About the couple you're staying with?" Gramp shook his head. "It's not the same thing at all. Family isn't people living together under one roof, no matter how fine and good they are to each other. Family is belonging — roots that go down into a very special and particular kind of soil. Soil with elements like loyalty, sharing — sharing both the joys and the sorrows, the good times and the bad. Give-and-take, now there's something you seldom get outside a strong family relationship. That total honesty that a person can depend upon receiving only from close ties.

A proper growth for the ego, taming some of the wild elements, the primitive hostility that lurks in all of us, shaving off the rough edges of the screaming, shouting, demanding, winner-take-all ego, yet nurturing it properly too. The 'I' is a tender plant, Shawn, and though it must be taught a proper degree of self-immolation, it must have strength of spirit pumped into it, the self-importance and self-worth that is the right of each and every one of us."

He paused, chuckled and said, "There, I've gone and rattled on like a gabby old man."

"Not at all, Gramp," Shawn told him.

Gramp pushed back his chair. "Before I wear out my welcome at this impromptu dinner party, I had better retire with good grace. Besides, it's time for the program I've been waiting for. I imagine you and Pete have things you can talk about without me."

Shawn helped her with the dishes. "This is fun," he said. "Mrs. Havens won't let me in the kitchen. She says it's woman's place and woman's work."

"Is that the way you feel about it, Shawn?"

He laughed. "Not me. I even like to cook. I used to at the last school I went to. There was this nutritionist who planned the meals, and she let some of the guys putter around the stove. We concocted some of the most god-awful messes you ever spit out of your mouth! But it was great. And I learned a couple of good recipes."

"Good. You can come over and take charge in Mom's kitchen. Me, I'm strictly an omelet-on-Saturday-morning cook. Eggs are my specialty. But Mom's an elegant chef and she'll adore having a man around to stir the pots. My brother Scott — the one who's in show business — used to have a knack with things like potato pancakes and goulash and something called a quiche, and chicken paprika."

"When do I begin?"

She grinned at him. "When you're invited."

"I hope that'll be soon."

"It will be. Gramp likes you."

"How can you tell?"

"The way he was shooting his mouth off about his favorite topics. And the way he pumped you about your own life."

"He's right about the latter. It's been bleak."

She gave him a quick look. "That doesn't mean it has to keep on being bleak." She felt the conversation might be getting too sticky on such short acquaintance, so she changed the subject. "How's your game going?"

"Basketball? I'll tell you better after tomorrow. We play our first big night game at Rockwood."

Pete rolled her eyes. "You have my condolences. They'll clobber you. They're the best in the state — they honestly are, the boys' team I mean, and the girls are no slouches either. If your team has been having trouble, Rockwood will have scouted you mercilessly and know all your weaknesses. That's the way they operate. Big-time stuff. No fooling around. A lot of Rockwood boys have made the headlines in basketball at college and some have even made it to the pros."

"So I've been told."

"Then why didn't you stop me five minutes ago? I don't like people who let you wander on while they're laughing up their sleeves because you're telling them old-hat tales. You've let me be a bore."

He came over, took the dish towel from her and tossed it on the table. He held her hands. "Pete, you'd never be a bore, never. I don't think there could ever be a dull moment with you." He leaned forward and kissed her, a quick kiss that somehow managed, for all its swiftness, to have a touch of tenderness and warmth.

"The door's open, and Gramp's chair is right in line with where we're standing," she told him.

"I have a feeling Gramp would heartily approve."

"And do you now? What makes you think so?"

"He left us alone, didn't he?"

"He said we'd have a lot to say to each other."

"Actions speak louder than words, and I've always considered myself a man of action." This time he put his arms around her, pulled her close, out of range of Gramp's vision, and gave her a more meaningful kiss.

She pushed him away. "Shawn, you're impossible."

"Why?"

"You just are, that's all. You're all charm and a yard wide. No wonder you're working wonders with the Bradford team morale. You do have a way with people."

"You've relieved my mind. I thought you might say I was too fresh."

"Why should I? We're an affectionate family. We kiss when we meet and when we leave each other. I was brought up with love, Shawn, lots of it, all around me. Plenty and to spare. So what's a kiss or two between friends?"

Shawn didn't answer right away. He walked over to a rack of books near the kitchen table and stood there thumbing the pages of one of them. So she was surprised when he came up behind and kissed the back of her neck saying, "I was hoping my kisses would mean more to you than 'a kiss or two between friends.'"

She wheeled on him. "Shawn, you are a charmer. Don't work your magic on me. I've been brought up to beware of those who kiss the Blarney stone."

"It's not blarney. I'm trying to tell you something."

"What?"

"That you're gentle on my mind. I can't stop thinking about you."

"Shawn, it's not right to say things like that when you can't possibly mean them."

"But I do mean them."

"We just met a few days ago, Shawn. We don't know anything much about each other."

"But it seems as if I've known you all my life. At first I couldn't understand it — what was happening — and then I knew. Every guy has a girl he thinks about as the kind of girl he might somehow, somewhere, sometime, meet. Not a dream girl, I don't mean anything as schmaltzy as that. I mean a girl a guy could enjoy being with a whole lot, and feel right with, comfortable and all that. No strain, no pretending to be something you aren't. A girl a guy could talk to about almost anything, about the things that mean the most to him, things deep inside him that he has always wanted to share with another human being but can't share with other guys."

"You are telling yourself that I'm all this?"

"I am telling myself that you could very well come to mean all this to me."

"You have a girl. You came to the Bradford game the other afternoon just to see Susan Alpert play. Everyone says she's your girl."

"We talked about that. I said I had one friend and now have another. Different people can mean different things to a guy."

"Since you bring the subject up, I'll ask you. What does she mean to you that I don't mean, and vice versa?"

"I don't like to discuss one friend with another."

"You are going to have to, Shawn. You started this serious conversation, and it is serious, believe me, and you are going to finish it or you'll never get to make potato pancakes in my mother's kitchen or eat cannelloni in Gramp O'Hara's place again."

"Okay. Here goes. But remember, you asked for it. Susan is special in her own way. She has a certain style. A sophistication I guess is what it is, savoir-faire about a lot of things. She's been around and has the poise to show for it. She's social. She likes to go. Dances, parties, people — these are the things Susan specializes in. She's vivacious and fun. Any guy would feel glad to be able to take her out."

"Then you're lucky she's latched on to you." Pete clapped her hand to her mouth. "There, I've done it again. Blurted out the way I think before weighing my words."

"I don't mind. Besides, you've overlooked what I'm trying to tell you. That some girls are froth and bubble and other girls are deep and serious."

"It's getting late, Shawn. I can hear that the program is changing. I'll bet Gramp's asleep." She walked to the living room door. "Sure enough. I'll wake him so he can say good-by."

"Don't disturb him, Pete."

"He'd never forgive us if I let you go without a parting word or two or five dozen!" She went in, tapped Gramp gently on the shoulder and said, "Shawn's just leaving. I'll walk out to his car with him and come back to say good night."

Her grandfather stood up and clasped Shawn's hand. "Come again, soon, Shawn. Next time I'll wait supper till you get here."

"Say, I've got a great idea, Gramp. Pete's team is playing Southport Friday night. Why don't I pick you up and we'll go together?" He turned to Pete. "Maybe your mother would like to come too."

"Friday is my brother Paul's night for having supper with Mom. My brothers take turns stopping by to cheer Mom up since Dad died."

"How about it, Gramp? Want to make it a family party?"

"Sure thing. It's a date."

Pete shrugged into her jacket and opened the door to a blast of winter air. "Whew, is it cold! I hope your car starts, Shawn."

"It will. I've got plenty of antifreeze."

As they crossed to where he had parked, Pete let out a shriek. "Hey, it's my new secondhand car. The one Paul left me for the old Mercedes. He must have brought it over while we were having supper. It's great having a brother in the secondhand car business! Look, Shawn, it's a Porsche! Shawn, come look. Isn't it the most? That Paul, he's the limit. Why didn't he tell me he was going to bring over a Porsche!" She fished in the glove compartment and found the keys Paul had left for her.

Shawn joined her, putting his arm around her waist as he said, "I can't wait for my first ride."

It was a cheerful, if speedy, good night they said as Shawn kissed her again before climbing into his sedan.

"You won't be speaking to us common folk now that you'll be riding around in a Porsche," he said with that humorous twist of the mouth.

"Think nothing of it," she told him. "A used car does not make the woman any more than hand-me-down clothes make the man."

She could hear his laughter follow her as she went back to say good night to Gramp. He was waiting for her in the kitchen. "I'm heating water. We'll have a hot drink before you leave."

"Better not. I'll take a rain check. Mom's due home any minute, and I don't like her to walk into an empty house, Gramp."

"Right you are. That's a fine young man you've got there, Pete."

"I haven't got him, Gramp. *He's* got *two* of us, a girl named Susan Alpert and me. Shawn thinks some girls are for fun and parties and other girls are deep and serious."

"Men settle down and marry the deep and serious ones."

"Now don't start that, Gramp. No one's thinking of marriage."

"Why not?"

"Because we're all too young and there are things like college education and careers to think about, that's why not."

"There's no harm in thinking and talking, is there?"

She went over and kissed him. "Gramp, sometimes your Irish really shows. You talk too much, but you've got the Irish charm."

"So has Shawn Patrick."

"That he has. He's a strange one, Gramp, don't forget it for one moment. He is that, a mighty strange guy. I haven't known him very long. First he submerges his male ego sufficiently to let me coach him in basketball. Now there's a foot in women's lib, if I ever heard of one. Then later he tells me off when we have lunch at the Friendly, warning me not to run down the place where I was born and raised by calling it, even humorously, The Bum Burg. Now today he hound-dogs me, coming here first, then trailing me to the school, then managing to get himself invited in for supper and to stay the evening."

"And he kissed you."

"You saw that, then?"

"You always said I have eyes in the back of my head."

"Yes. But what is much worse, he talked seriously about things I didn't even understand. About having always dreamed about a girl he would meet whom he could be with all the time and feel great with, and he said he felt as if he had known me all his life because I was that girl. But right on top of that he explained Susan Alpert to me. What she does for him, how special she is in her own way. And that certainly is *not* having one foot in women's lib! Two girls for every man!" She shuddered. "The Greeks might have a word for it, but I'm sure any red-blooded American girl would not!"

"Still, he's a fine young man, and I'll say it again if I must in order to have myself heard and understood plainly, my girl."

"I understood the first time, Timothy O'Hara. Now I'll speak my own mind, if you please. Sure and he's a fine young man, but he's also a guy to beware of. Gramp, I think Shawn Patrick could be dynamite. He moves in too fast. He takes over. And he's desperately lonely."

"What has loneliness got to do with the rest of it?"

"Desperately lonely people are Venus fly-traps."

"That plant which, when its delicate hairs are touched, snaps like a trap?"

"That's right. Some lonely people do that to the people they get close to and want. They trap and possess you."

"I think you're making too much of a few kisses and a couple of paragraphs of talk."

"We'll see about that," she said. "Good night and sweet dreams, and don't lose any sleep over my problems."

"That I won't, my girl. That I will never do."

He stood at the door of the cottage, waving as she crossed over to the big house. She was thinking. About two men, really. That was the strange thing about it. Although she had spent the entire evening with Shawn and enjoyed him very much, she had not quite put Burt Johnson out of her thoughts. He was there. Not just the hassle with him, or the rough exchange of words, or the needling, or her dislike. Something else. The whole long stretch of the man. The slender, muscular, Indian frame. The way he moved, quickly and quietly, so that he could come up behind a player on the basketball court and you could not hear him. The face with the bold aggressive features, handsome, slightly mocking. The strength of the man. The eyes that bored through you and seemed to see things you did not even know about yourself.

That was one of the men on her mind.

And the other was Shawn. *That* Shawn. That guy who could move in and take over and do it quickly and make you laugh at everything he did or said and love him for it. A sweet guy with what Gramp called "the Irish ferment in the soul." Restlessness. Unpredictability. A touch of mystery.

Two men. Both on her mind. Both exciting and dangerous, each in his own way. As she opened the back door, her mother's car spit over the tarmac drive. Pete went on into the house, thinking, A week ago I had no man to think about and tonight I have two!

Later, upstairs, Pete thought about it all. She seldom spent much time gawking in the mirror, but she stared at herself now. She thought about Susan Alpert, Shawn's "friend." Even in the Bradford basketball tunic, which did little for the girls who wore them, Susan managed to be quite a beauty. She was dark, with delicate features and wide-set golden-brown eyes, well fringed with naturally heavy lashes. So Pete spent an unusual amount of time in taking stock of her own appearance.

Nothing delicate about you, Petrina, she said silently to her reflection. You're out of the competition before you start.

She was a big girl — tall, strong of frame, large-boned. Connie kept telling her she had a great figure and Pete would laugh it off, but now she turned this way and that and guessed that Connie might be right. The proportions were good, providing you would settle for a gal not the least bit skimpy!

In summer her hair was the color of ripe wheat, but come fall it began to look dark and drab. She never did anything to it but trim it herself and wash it a couple of times a week, under the shower — none of this fussing with rinses and stuff as Connie and the others did. The one good thing about her hair was that it had body. She could push and shove it anyway she wanted and, presto, it stayed there!

Hair was one thing you could shift around a bit, but a face was something else again. Pete regretted hers. It had been called things like "wholesome" and "open," and it was. It gave away every single thing she thought about anything and everybody. The eyes looked straight on, direct, probing, a blinding blue. The mouth was wide and expressive. It smiled a lot. The nose was too big, she thought, although Gramp said it went with the rest of her.

"A strong nose shows intelligence," he had told her.

"It also gets in the way of basketballs and arms that hack on the court," she had replied.

Now she shrugged at her image and said aloud, "Susan, old gal, you've got nothing to worry about."

CHAPTER THREE

In this zero hour before the start of the South-port game, Pete's senses were painfully sharpened. Familiar symptom! she thought. It did not matter which gym she was playing in. The same heightened awareness assailed her before every important contest, but especially a night game.

Since the Southport team was still down in their locker room, the Central High girls had the spanking-new Southport gym to themselves for their warm-up. Pete practiced passes with Camilla Gomez. Dribbling the length of the court, she hurled a high hook pass.

Too high, she thought, as Camilla ran, jumped, missed. That was my fault, not Camilla's. I'm as taut as a caged animal. Let go, gal. Loosen up. But that's easier said than done.

Pete could not follow her own excellent advice. Every sound grated. The PA system rattled off a test spiel while the noisy crowd of spectators poured through the wide doors, filling up the stands.

Pete kept moving, dribbling, and passing to Camilla, then running back to receive the return pass. She missed too many.

Someone on the Southport side shouted, "Hey, Phillips, don't wear yourself out. You'll need all the pep you've got when the Southport team shows up."

It was good-natured banter, but it touched a nerve.

"Hold it," she called to Camilla. "I'm soaking wet." Stopping by the substitute bench, she grabbed a towel and mopped up. As she tossed the towel back to their manager, Meg Mumford, Pete grumbled, "There's too much heat in this place. It's like a greenhouse. What do they think they're doing, growing orchids!"

Meg Mumford grinned and said, "They should make allowances for pregame jitters."

Pete moved down to the end of the bench, not answering. Meg's right, she thought. It's not the temperature, it's me. Whew, I'm all nerves. And I've got that dry, metallic taste in my mouth.

Pete had experienced this special "court fright" before, but tonight it seemed sharper, more insistent. She decided to concentrate on the scene around her in order to submerge her self-consciousness. Her eyes traveled up to the huge pep signs that some energetic Southport fans had stretched across the walls of their gym. CLOBBER CENTRAL. GO, GERTIE, GO. SINK THEM, STROBIE. Gertie was Gertrude Hemming and Strobie was Pat Strobemeyer, the two high scorers on the Southport Five. And that brought Pete's thoughts right straight back to her problems.

No wonder I've got pregame jitters, she thought, facing two of the county's best shooters, with a right hand that's gone temperamental. That made her think of Burt Johnson and what he had told them: *Every game is for winning*.

Don't think about Burt, she warned herself. You're upset enough without worrying about the way you haven't been hitting it off with him this past week.

It had been a silent battle between them — Burt giving plenty of attention and help to the other girls while he ignored Pete, and Pete withdrawing stubbornly into her shell, pretending that she didn't care.

Southport had imported two big-name coaches from the Midwest.

At first everyone had said it would never work, that this was not the Midwest where girls' basketball was so big that it often overshadowed the boys' game. "You'll never get the local girls to play that kind of hard-driving, tough, clobbering game," one news commentator had said. But he was wrong. Ted Evans and Lucy Betts had not only got the Southport girls to play "that kind of game," they had pulled the entire area into the competition. It was these two coaches, Evans and Betts, who, several years back, had initiated the night games for girls' teams. And now that the girls' rules practically equaled the boys, the games were tough and competitive. No more ballet on the court.

As Burt Johnson had reminded the Central High girls on that first day he coached them, every game is for blood or it's not worth playing.

Pete took her place in the lineup for shots at the basket. Ahead of her were Connie and Bretta, the other two Central High forwards, and behind her were Camilla Gomez, Tammy Kovacks, Jinnie Lawson, the three who played guard. At the tail end were Joan Redford and Kim Kyser, the two most active substitutes. Angie Alvieri, who was the tallest girl on the team and played center, stood under the bucket to toss the ball and catch rebounds.

Connie sank a shoulder shot. Bretta tried a jump shot and missed. Then came Pete's turn. Her hands were moist. She rubbed them on her shorts. She had no idea what her wrist was going to do for or against her tonight. The past week, since the day when Burt Johnson had given her a dose of what she preferred to call "amateur psychology," she had been in a state of panic every time she went into a practice game there at the Central High gym or down in Bamberger Hall. The worst part of it was Burt Johnson's attitude toward her. He let her strictly alone. Throughout the week he had concentrated on shaping up the rest of the team. He had gotten results: Bretta was keeping her mouth shut — if not entirely, at least noticeably. Connie wasn't pushing so hard. Camilla had "stirred her stumps" and was moving faster. Tammy was still no Bill Russell so far as shots were concerned, but she was working at it, and although Jinnie would never win a medal for self-assertiveness, there was some improvement.

Yessir, Burt had worked on all the girls, except Pete. In fact, he had not spoken a half dozen sentences to her since that afternoon when she had turned off his attempt to help her.

So she had struggled through the week, not knowing where she was heading. Her wrist — or at least she blamed her wrist — was totally unpredictable. One day she would miss half her shots, another day she would make almost all of them. There was just no telling what or when. So this warm-up was important to Pete.

"Let's try for quick shots, Pete!" Angie Alvieri held the ball high for a pass. Pete felt the whack as it hit her hands. She ran toward the keyhole intending to try for an easy lay-up. But she was in too much of a hurry — her foot skidded and she had to pivot and dribble before she could try for a shot. That spoiled her plan for a lay-up and she held the ball toward her shoulder for a shot straight off the arm. It sailed high — a neat, steady arc. She knew it was good. She had not lost that knack of being able to tell, the second the ball left her hands, whether the shot would be good or bad. She watched the ball roll around the rim. Not as clean as she would have liked. But it did sink in. She hoped it was an omen. Maybe it was.

She took her place in the lineup again. Again she sank her shot. Someone patted her on the shoulder. It was Connie. "Nice going, Pete. Keep it up."

If I can, she thought, if I only can.

The PA cut into her thoughts. "Your attention, please. The Southport team is now coming on the floor. Let's give them a hand." Loud cheering, horns, noisemakers, yells. Cheerleaders running out, flouncing their short skirts and waving their megaphones. The big gym shook with Southport cheers.

The Southport girls went quietly to their end of the gym and started shooting in a brief intense warm-up. Pete turned and watched. She sucked in her breath. They were terrific. You couldn't tell the forwards from the guards, not by the way they made baskets. Their shots were spectacular and deadly accurate.

Another blast from the PA system. "The lineup for this evening's game. For Central High:

Forwards, Pete Phillips and Bretta Masi. Guards, Camilla Gomez and Tammy Kovacks. Center, Angie Alvieri.

"For Southport High: Forwards, Gert Hemming and Strobie Strobemeyer. Guards, Midge Madison and Pat Wentworth. Center, Lynn Dumont."

There was a short pause, then the PA blared forth again. "Ladies and Gentlemen: our national anthem."

Pete stood at attention with her team as the loudspeaker blared "The Star-spangled Banner." Then she hurried to the floor with her co-captain, Camilla Gomez, to listen to the officials rattle off the rules, and to go through the ceremony of basket-choosing and handshaking with the captains of the Southport team.

She ran to take her place with her team. The whistle blew, the ball went up for the tip-off. The game was on.

Lynn Dumont won the jump for Southport and Midge Madison was there to catch it. The ball went in accurate passes from Midge to Pat, back to Midge, on to Lynn, who sent it to Gert Hemming.

She'll try for an overhead, Pete thought, seeing that her own guards, Camilla and Tammy, were on the job blocking an easy shot at the basket.

Gert feinted right, left, right again as if to make the try for a fast overhead shot. This strategy brought Bretta Masi and Angie Alvieri joining the two Central High guards in a rectangle at the Southport keyhole.

Pete wanted to shout, Watch it, kids. Don't do that! She didn't have time for even a signal, because Gert sent the ball over her shoulder in a backhand pass. It plunked into Strobie's waiting hands. Pete, detecting the deceptive play, was moving hard toward Strobie. She was too late to do anything but damage. Pete's arm banged Strobie's elbow as the Southport forward aimed for the hoop. Despite the interference, Strobie, so near the basket she could have breathed into it, arced the ball in a clean lay-up.

The referee's whistle blew, and he held up his fist and indicated a hacking foul. The stands came into the act, roaring their approval at the official's decision. The Southport cheerleaders were out on the floor, shouting through their horns, "Okay, let's give Southport a cheer for a fast start. One, two, three . . ."

Pete turned her back on the roaring crowd, hiked up her shorts, and ground her teeth. She was staring straight into the Central High side of the stands. Down front, there was a slight commotion. She saw that it was caused by two late arrivals, Paul and her mother, finding their places as they squeezed in next to Gramp and Shawn Patrick.

Shawn waved to Pete as the voice on the PA boomed, "Personal foul on Pete Phillips, Central High, for hacking."

The teams lined up at the free-throw line. Strobie caught the ball tossed to her by the official. She bounced it a few times, toed up to the line, and aimed. The shot was good. The scoreboard flashed: Southport 3, Visitors 0.

The ball was Central High's. Angie took it out-of-bounds, and the game was on again — no time for recriminations. Angie sent the ball to Bretta. Bretta jumped for the catch and started a dribbling drive in for the basket. Pete caught a signal from Bretta and started for the Central High keyhole, making it before the Southport team could turn its attention toward her. Southport was double-teaming on their defense to block Bretta. She had to pass off. Pete was too far away. Bretta tossed it to the only Central High girl in the clear, Camilla Gomez.

Camilla dribbled, looking for a teammate who could receive a pass. Pete signaled Camilla to let Tammy have the ball. Camilla used a hand-off pass at close quarters, her weight low and her knees bent. It worked. Tammy got her hands on the side of the ball, held on to it, and dribbled, looking for a chance to pass the ball to Angie. Angie, the tallest girl on the team, got the pass and signaled Tammy for a zigzag attack. The two of them kept the ball going back and forth between them in a series of lightning passes, while Pete tried to stay loose from the Southport defense. The ball zoomed at her straight from Tammy's hands. Pete ran to meet it, jumped, and felt it whack into her upstretched fingers. Her glance darted, birdlike, for a safe shot. Southport's zone defense was coming straight for her.

She thought, No time or room for a hook shot. It's got to be a quick pivot or a jump shot. I'll fake it. It's my best chance.

Pete pivoted, feinted, jumped, and let the ball go. It sailed straight for the center of the backboard, exactly where she had planned. It banked and tumbled through the hoop.

Southport 3, Central High 2.

Midge Madison took the ball out for Southport and they began their powerful drive down the court toward their own basket. This time there was no need for the strategy of breaking up the Central High defense. Southport played it their own way. They fed the ball to Strobie, who sank it easily. Pete was not within several yards of her. There was no fouling on the shot.

Southport 5, Central High 2.

When Angie took the ball out for Central High, Bretta clapped her hands for the pass but she missed it. Gert Hemming caught the fumble and headed for the Southport basket. Angie was there ahead of her, blocking Gert's shot. Gert had to get rid of it. Once again she had to pass off to Strobie, who sank it, using a safe one-handed set shot.

Southport 7, Central High 2.

Miss Loudon called time-out for Pete's team.

Pete nudged her way into the huddle. She was glad it was Miss Loudon's huddle and not Burt Johnson's. Pete did not hear a word of what the Central High coach said during the brief pep talk. She didn't have to hear it. Miss Loudon had been using the same one for over twenty years. The girls liked Miss Loudon. She was friendly and pleasant to work with. But her pep talks about cooperation and alertness were not what had won games for the girls of Central High. What had won the ghetto girls their trophies was their drive, their shrewdness and guts, their competitive intuition, all gained from having grown up in the "street."

While Miss Loudon sweet-talked the team, Pete's mind sized up the Southport game, its style and strategy.

Strobie, Pete thought. Strobie's the clue to

this game. Any player who gets three goals early in the game is going to hang on to that ball every chance she gets. She'll forget about throwing it to her teammates. She'll cage that ball herself every time. Tonight the hot hand on the ball is Strobie's. Nobody, but nobody, will get the chance to keep her from smashing records.

Pete thought, I think that tells me what to do.

She fell into step with Angie Alvieri as they returned to their positions. Angie was a first-class playmaker. Also, she would not forget that Pete had covered for her when she was note-passing to Herb Weston the other day in Mrs. Byrd's class.

"Angie, Strobemeyer's the key. She'll sink that ball every chance she gets. You're the tallest girl on the team. Glue yourself to Strobie and stay as close as you can without bringing the referee's whistle down on you. Then bring that ball to me. I'll play like I was an old-fashioned post player, something Southport would never expect."

"Pete, you're flaky. They'll pour it on you, using straight zone defense, box you in, block your shots, and maybe cripple you in the bargain."

"Let me worry about that. You muzzle Strobemeyer and get that ball to me."

"It's your picnic, Pete."

"Angie, one other thing. I fouled Strobie because I remembered too late that she's left-handed. So press her from a spot that will block her left-handed shots. If you force her to shoot from the position of a right-handed player, you just might jinx that hot hand. When she misses,

34

be sure to get the rebound." Pete clapped a hand on Angie's shoulder and grinned. "Bon voyage."

Pete kept her eye on Angie as the ball went into play. Angie had listened well. She lost no chance to block Strobie's shots and get the ball to Pete. If Pete's hand was not quite so hot as Strobie's, it wasn't lukewarm either. Pete sank her shots. No one seemed to notice that she had to use a lot of two-handed set shots. What mattered was the score. At the end of the first quarter it stood 20-9 in favor of Central High. Pete had sunk nine of the ten baskets for Central, and Bretta had made the other goal. Gert Hemmings had racked up the extra two points for Southport when she aimed from dead-center court with a spectacular shot that brought the stands to their feet.

The horn sounded the end of the quarter. It had been a rough eight minutes of play. Both teams were winded. Strobie looked spooked.

The Southport coach, Ted Evans, went into the two-minute huddle with his frustrated team. Pete watched. She thought, Evans is telling them to get the devil in there and take that ball away from Phillips and pull Alvieri off Strobemeyer's back. The next quarter will be an interesting bout!

The second quarter began the way the first had ended, with Angie playmaking for Central and keeping the ball away from Strobie, while the girls from Bamberger Village made a fast break down the court to their waiting post player at the keyhole. In the first minute and a half of play Pete made another two baskets, racking up four points on field goals plus two more for free throws, because Pat Wentworth fouled Pete in the act of shooting a third basket and the ball missed the rim.

The scoreboard read: Southport 9, Visitors 26.

Ted Evans called time-out the minute his girls got their hands on the ball.

When Southport came back into the game, it was with a difference. Midge Madison was out. A burly "hatchetman" of a guard, Biffer Rissuto, was in. Biffer's real name was Marilyn, but no one remembered. Biffer had "killer instinct." Used only for tight spots, she was awesome window dressing sprawled on the Southport bench, the six-feet, two-hundred-pound brawn of her, the slab of face, pudgy nose, and slits of eyes. To have Biffer sent into the game this early in the second quarter was so unprecedented that it sent nervous flurries through the Central High team. She was usually saved for fourth quarter emergencies when she was used at all.

Angie sidled up to Pete and muttered, "What's Biffer being sent in for?"

"Me," was Pete's laconic reply.

On the first play, Pete saw that Southport had switched from zone defense to man-to-man. She thought, So it's to be one-on-one and I've struck the jackpot — Biffer Rissuto.

For the first couple of minutes, the Southport change of strategy worked well for them. Biffer, past master in the art of kneeing, elbowing, ribbing, without bringing the whistle down on her, managed to give Pete plenty of lumps. The Southport defense rallied, turned offensive for a power drive toward their basket, and Strobie and Gert shoveled the ball into the Southport bucket. They scored eight points before the Central High team had time to catch their breath.

Pete asked for time-out. Miss Loudon stayed off the court and Pete gathered the girls around her. She was puffing hard from Biffer's last rib-thrust. Bent over and holding her side, she kept her voice pitched to a throaty whisper.

"They've got me hog-tied. Someone else has to do the shooting. How about you, Bretta?"

"I can't," Bretta said. "I can't get near the keyhole. Pat Wentworth is their tallest, and they've put her on me. She's a regular leech."

"She's also overeager."

"I don't read you, Pete," Bretta said.

"You only have to get her to foul you once more. She's got two fouls called on her already. Ted Evans will take her out after three fouls. That's too much too soon. He'll need to save her for the last half of the game."

"How do I get her to foul me?"

Pete grinned. "You're asking me? *Talk* her into it, Big Mouth. Needle her, like you do everyone else."

"What about?"

"Anything you can think of," Pete said. "You're the expert!"

"Then what happens?" Bretta asked.

"With Pat out, the substitute guard won't be so tough to cope with. You'll be free. They've put their weakest player on Angie in the man-to-man switcheroo. So you two will have the basket. Sink shots as fast as you can get your hands on the ball. Bretta, use your set shot.

Angie, you can lay them up nice and easy once you get near the basket. No problem. Okay?"

The girls nodded as the horn called them back to the game.

It worked. Pete watched Bretta get to work on Pat Wentworth. Bretta's mouth was going a mile a minute. The result was not one, but two fouls called on Pat within half a minute of play. She went out and Deedie Albertson came in. Deedie looked worried as she reported to the scorer's table.

Good, Pete thought. A worried guard is a cautious guard.

The tempo of the game changed. Once again Central High got possession and managed to keep the ball. Within the last few minutes of the second quarter Bretta and Angie were able to rack up five goals. Southport made one more point on a free throw when Camilla got moving too fast and had a foul called against her for tripping up Gert Hemming.

The scoreboard flashed Southport 18, Visitors 36, as the horn ended the first half of the game. The girls got out fast. Pete lagged behind, stopping to say a quick hello to her family. Then she moved out and pushed her way through the crowd that milled out into the foyer. She ran down the stairs to the locker rooms. The Central High room was a madhouse, a lot of shouting and gloating. The girls felt pretty good. An eighteen-point lead will do that to a team in a big game, Pete thought. You forget it's not over.

She listened to the sounds from the Southport locker room. It was startlingly quiet compared with the bedlam in the Central High headquarters. She could hear Ted Evans' voice, steady, low-pitched, but she couldn't hear what he was saying.

If he's furious— and he ought to be, she thought — he's certainly hiding it.

Miss Loudon was fluttering among her brood, patting shoulders and backs, supervising manager Meg Mumford as she applied Band-Aids. Pete separated herself from the crowd. She liked a bit of solitude in the ten minutes between halves. It was a good time to think about what had been happening up there on the court. And she had something to think about. Something she couldn't talk over with anyone.

Her wrist had done that "thing" again. In the last few seconds of play just before the intermission, the ball had come zooming at her over Biffer Rissuto's head and she had jumped for it, pivoted, and tried for a basket. She had missed some other shots too. But differently. Not because of that twist in her wrist. She had almost forgotten about it until that last shot at the basket.

Then there it was again. It worried her.

She went out to get a drink of water and when she returned from the fountain she saw him. He was standing in the doorway. Not moving. Just looking. Burt Johnson.

She decided to go on up to the gym and avoid the rush. The back door is the easiest way, she thought. Then I won't have to pass him. When she stepped out into the hall, there he was, standing directly in her path. He had moved so quickly and silently that he startled her. They stood there alone, looking at each other.

"You played well," he told her. She started past him and again he blocked her path. "I came to warn you," he went on. "You'll have something besides the Southport team to buck during the last half."

"Which means?"

"You'll have the mood of the stands. The spectators will come into the game. They'll psych you, or try to. I know this crowd — from way back, I know them. This school wants to win. It has to win. Central High has always been their closest rival, and what they like next best to winning is for their closest rival to lose."

"I'm used to heckling from the stands," she told him.

"I'm not talking about heckling," he said. "I'm talking about blood. The Southport fans will want blood, Pete. Yours. You're the star, Pete. That's the price you pay. My advice to you is to keep your cool. Turn a deaf ear to the stands. Don't listen. It will take guts."

"Thanks," she said. "Thanks for nothing." She ran past him and up the stairs to the gym. Burt Johnson made her churn inside. After a week of silence, she thought, now he gives advice — almost friendly.

When the second half began, Southport had once again made some changes. Biffer was out. Midge Madison and Pat Wentworth were both back in the game. Central High had also made some changes. Connie was in for Bretta Masi and Tammy was on the bench, with Jinnie Lawson taking her place as guard. Pete tallied up the effect of these changes on the Central High potential. Connie had more speed than Bretta.

But while her size might be advantageous in fast passes, it could hamper her in getting the ball past tall guards for shots at the hoop. Jinnie was an above-average shooter but she played a defensive game and was more interested in keeping the ball from Southport than in sinking it herself.

On the first play, Pete saw how right Burt Johnson's analysis had been. Strobie fouled. "Charging!" the referee called, extending his palms. The stands booed. Their protests shook the rafters. When Pete took the ball for the free throw and missed, the Southport fans howled their delight. A few seconds later, Strobie held the ball high for a center-court hook shot, made it and scored two points. The Southport rooters rose, screaming their approval. The gym was wild with cheers. It was like nothing Pete had ever heard before.

The shouts and screams bordered on pandemonium.

The noise and the confusion were so great that Pete could not keep track of what was happening. She found herself going through the motions of the game, automatically, unable to keep her mind on the action. She did what she had to do. Caught the ball, tried for shots, dribbled, pivoted, but she felt as if she were not with it — that it was happening to someone else.

They're psyching us, she thought. Burt Johnson was right. They're psyching us, but good!

The third quarter ended with the score 40-40.

It was obvious that the ball had remained largely in Southport's possession throughout the quarter. Southport had made nine baskets and racked up four points at the free-throw line. Central High's two goals had been made by Connie Anderson. Pete had not been near enough to the ball to get her hands on it more than twice. Both times she had passed off to Connie.

In the brief rest between quarters, she lay face down on the floor, thinking, wondering. She could hear Miss Loudon's voice droning away. This time she turned a deaf ear for a far different reason than during the early part of the game. This time she was frightened. Of something nameless. No, it wasn't nameless. She knew what she was frightened of. She was afraid of herself.

I'm running scared, she thought. I'm afraid to shoot. That's why I'm not getting my hands on the ball and why I'm passing off every chance I get. *I'm afraid to try for a basket.*

The horn called them back into the game.

She listened to the noise in the stands as the ball went into play. It was still a furor. For the first five minutes of play the ball did a seesaw. Bretta was back in the game and she was keyed up, ready for action. Bretta and Jinnie kept the score evened up. First Southport would score a goal, then Central High would put one through the hoop. The horn warned that it was the last two minutes of play. Pete glanced at the scoreboard.

56-55 in favor of Southport.

It was Southport's ball. It went to Strobie at center court. Pete figured Strobie would try for a long shot. She didn't. She waited too long, giving the Central High guards time to move in and block. Strobie had to pass. She sent the ball to Gert Hemming, who took it almost under the board. Gert tried for what looked like a sure shot. The ball teetered on the rim. It rolled off. A howl of dismay went up from the Southport stands.

The cheerleaders bounced out on the floor.

"Go, Southport, go! Make that goal. Sink the next one."

Angie got the rebound from Gert Hemming's miss. She started dribbling down the court toward the Central High basket. Through the confusion in the gym it was hard to hear the voices from the Central High side, but a few came through to Pete.

"Make it, Angie." "Shoot, Angie. Shoot!"

With Southport leading by one point, Angie had to do something and do it fast. She had a choice. To try to shoot for a goal or to pass the ball off to someone in a better position to hit the target. It was a tough decision to make. Angie hefted the ball, flicking her glance around the court, looking for the right teammate to receive the ball.

Pete faded away from the bucket. Don't send it to me, her thoughts shouted. Pass it to anyone else. Not me!

Angie held the ball high for a two-handed sidearm pass. She faked with her eyes, as if to send the ball to Bretta. Then she swerved and released it. The ball came straight at Pete.

Automatically Pete's hands went up as she jumped to receive the pass. She caught the ball easily, holding it loosely between her fingers. She smelled the rubber, the heat, the sweat. She listened to the noise from the stands. A sharp stab of anger rose inside her.

She tightened her grip on the ball, a hard fast clutch that was not any good. She tried to loosen her fingers and couldn't. Suddenly there was silence in the gym — a terrifying silence as the spectators became quiet with the tension of suspense.

Pete could hear two things in that interim of silence. Her own heartbeat and the tick of the clock. Three seconds to go. She was a mechanical doll. A robot. A machine. She kept her eyes on the spot on the backboard where she intended to bank a shot. She kept her left foot in front, ready to hook the ball with her right hand. Bringing her right leg up, she pivoted off the cushion of her left foot and released the ball as she turned toward the basket, her left hand high for protection as she let go.

She watched the ball drop through the hoop as the horn ended the game.

The scoreboard flashed the victory for Central High.

Southport 56, Visitors 57.

Pete stood riveted to the spot from which she had hooked her winning shot. She listened to the sounds in the gym. The band striking up a march. The crowd milling out. The chatter, the voices shouting.

One lone voice, a resonant one, got through to Pete.

"Phillips, this was your lucky night. You lost your grip in the last half, Phillips. You're slipping."

Inside her was a strange emptiness that did

not fit the mood of victory, the satisfaction she should be feeling over having made that final winning goal.

She was upset. Not because of the heckler. She had heard that kind of sour grapes before. That was not what disturbed her. It was something much more significant than a sorehead loser venting his spleen on the player who had tossed in the winning shot.

She knew the fear that was inside her. She knew the narrow margin of confidence on which she had tossed that last shot. Her knees were still rubber. Her hands trembled. There was sweat on her palms and a tight knot in the back of her neck.

The guy is right, she thought. That final basket was plain luck. It was not finesse or skill or control or any of the things it should have been.

CHAPTER FOUR

Central High played two games the next week. They were afternoon games against minor teams in the league. Tuesday they met Clifton, a home game for Central High played to a small group of spectators in their own gym. On Thursday they traveled by chartered bus over to Ash Creek.

They lost to Clifton with a score of 40-36. At Ash Creek they squeaked an uneasy victory with a score of 30-28 against a team of girls who were short-statured, young, and inexperienced — not anywhere near being the athletes that the Central High girls were supposed to be.

Pete did not have to be told what the trouble was. She was continuing to do what she had done in the last half of the Southport game. She was running scared. She was passing the ball every chance she got. When she did try for a goal, her hand did that strange little twist and she would miss almost every time.

Although Miss Loudon attended both games, she relegated the coaching duties to Burt Johnson. "It's good practice for a student teacher," she explained to the girls on the team. "And besides, these games don't count for the league championships."

Burt had little to say to Pete during either game. After the Ash Creek contest, his car was parked close to the school exit, so she had to pass it when she hurried toward the chartered bus.

"Pete," he called. "Pete Phillips." She stopped and turned. He beckoned to her and called, "I've got permission to give you a ride home. It's okay. I've checked with Miss Loudon."

She walked slowly back toward his Volkswagen. "How come?"

"I think it's time we had a talk." She hesitated, making no move to get in. He opened the door. "It's all right, Pete. Miss Loudon knows about it." She shrugged and got in.

He turned the car out onto the main highway and headed back toward Bradford. Snow had started to fall, a light moist snow that was not sticking. After a couple of miles, she said, "So talk."

"Later," he told her. "This stuff is slippery. I've got to watch the road and the other cars."

She didn't answer. She felt uneasy. It didn't make any sense. Not at all. She knew she had played a lousy game both times this week. She knew what the trouble was. She had basket-phobia, a not uncommon affliction. She didn't need Burt Johnson to tell her what was the matter with her game.

Keep your mouth shut, she told herself. Let this guy do the talking. Listen but don't talk. He's just a guy trying to get a degree to teach physical ed. So let him get his diploma and go off to Kalamazoo to do his thing. Don't mess around with him or his ideas. Just listen.

When they reached the outskirts of Bradford, he pulled over to the side of the road and turned toward her.

"It's past suppertime for both of us. You must be as hungry as I am. How about having a talk over a hamburger?"

"My brother Scott's coming to supper tonight. He can make it only about once a month. I like to be home when he's there."

"Scott's gone into show business, hasn't he?"

"Right now he's directing for public television."

"Scott always was a talented guy. I like him."

"The compliment wasn't necessarily returned."

She could see the faint flicker of a smile cross his face. "Now that we've got the cards on the table," he replied with more good nature than she had a right to expect, "maybe you'll feel better about accepting my hospitality. I'll promise to get you back early enough to have plenty of time with Scott. How about it?"

"I'd have to call home and see how Mom feels about it."

"There's a booth just ahead. Need a dime?"

"I've got my own." When she dialed, her mother told her to go ahead, Scott had called and said he would be late and he planned to stay over anyway. "Gramp's coming over too. We'll save dessert, Pete. So go and have a good time."

When she got back to the car, she said, "I'll have to be home by eight at the latest."

"Will do," Burt said. He took her to a little restaurant called the Brick Wall. It was a tea-room, sedate and square, and Burt's choice of place surprised Pete — as did the solicitousness with which he ordered for her. She grudgingly acknowledged his social poise.

"What did you want to talk about?" she asked him point-blank as she shifted uneasily, waiting for him to begin.

"I've been watching your game closely, Pete. You've got a problem. A big one."

"Tell me something I don't know."

"I want to talk about helping you with it."

"Helping me! Of course I was only a kid with a dirty face when you messed up the boys' basketball team. But you'll have to excuse me if I say I don't recall that you had a reputation for helping — anyone with anything."

"What you're telling me is that the Burt Johnson you remembered was a troublemaker."

"Something along those lines."

He didn't answer at once. He stared off into the distance. When he turned to her, his eyes had softened.

"You're right," he said. "I was a troublemaker. But has it occurred to you, Pete, that people change? That time and experience can do things to a person so he isn't what he was once?"

"Maybe we should get back on the subject," she told him. "My basketball game. I can sum it up in two words. It smells. To high heaven, it smells. Tuesday I was terrible and today I was worse, and even last Friday evening when I heaved in that final shot and racked up quite a few points early in the game I still wasn't all that brilliant. I was moving along on nerve and gall. Strobie Strobemeyer was the gal with the hot hand on the ball. What I had was two sweaty palms and a parcel of luck."

"That isn't strictly an accurate report, Pete."

"What is an accurate report then? You give it to me."

"I'm not sure I can, at this point anyway. But one thing I know is that you are an exceptional player, a real basketball ace."

"Come off it. I've been a dud this season, and everyone knows it."

"Let me finish. I also think you're a girl very much in need of help. As I said before, I'd like to help you."

"How?"

"By setting up some private practice sessions."

"Where?"

"In Bamberger Hall. It's practically a haunted house — seldom used. But old Mr. Bamberger pays for the fuel and the custodian, so the place is available. I'd like to begin the sessions tomorrow. Right after school, unless you have something else more important."

"Nothing is more important than basketball," she told him.

Having won his point, he did not press the issue and that was shrewd of him. Because she was anything but sold on the idea, and if he had not been smart enough to hold his tongue once he had the upper hand, she would have backed out, quickly and happily. She didn't want Burt Johnson's assistance. She was not running to grab at his offer. She couldn't even understand why she agreed, unless it was because inside her burned a kind of desperation. After the games with Clifton and Ash Creek, she would have been willing to try anything that would pull her out of the shooting doldrums.

As he got up and helped her on with her coat, she asked him the question uppermost in her mind, "Do you think anything will help?"

His answer was honest. "I don't know," he said. "I'd be a liar if I said I was sure the practice sessions will pay off. Frankly, I don't know. All we can do is try."

On the way home he was his usual silent self.

TAB
FIC   W14g

He pulled into Pete's driveway near the side door. "Back safe and sound," he said, "and nice and early too. See you tomorrow, Pete. I'll be there waiting." He reached over to open the door for her. His hand brushed her arm and shoulder. She drew back. Then she jumped out, called a quick good night, and ran for the back door. She could hear Scott, Gramp, and Mom talking a blue streak. She held back, hoping they had not heard her. She needed time to pull herself together. She felt as she had the other night at the game in Southport — upset by the personality of this guy, by the "something" that stirred within her whenever Burt talked to her. She could not understand it. She was afraid to wonder about it, afraid of what she might find out about herself, not about Burt Johnson, but about herself.

"Pete, is that you?" It was her mother. They had heard her stomping around in the vestibule. "Scott's here, Pete."

"I'll be right in."

Scott got up. He stood beside his chair. She looked at him. It had been a month, perhaps longer, since he had been able to make his "Thursday night supper with Mom." He looked marvelous. A bit tired, but otherwise wonderful. Not huge like Tim, but big enough. And handsome, how breathtakingly handsome! The blinding blue eyes, the fair hair, the firm even features, the thrust of chin and jaw, the smile.

"Scott, it's really you!" He opened his arms, and she ran into them. He held her close a long minute of time that stood still for her, a time of safety and belonging, of understanding and love.

TRINIDAD HIGH SCHOOL
LIBRARY

3138

"I've brought you a present, Pete." He turned and fished something from his flight bag. She could hear him winding it up. It sounded like a mechanical toy. He set it on the table and she and Gramp and Mom gathered around to take a look. It was a small doll, a girl in a green basketball tunic, holding a basketball over her head, then thrusting it out in what might have been a hook shot.

"Scott, it's absolutely out of sight! Where did you get it?"

"A flea market in the Midwest."

Gramp was chuckling. "That doll's the spitting image of Pete. Light hair, blue eyes, same coloring."

"Gramp's right, Pete," Scott agreed. "She does look quite a bit like you. And the tunic is green and white, the colors of Central High. Isn't it a gas?"

"Scott, you had it made specially. You did now, I'm sure."

"No, honestly. I just stumbled on it. One night after a real crazy rehearsal when nothing had gone right, a couple of my pals and I went out to forget our troubles. And we stumbled into this flea market and there was this player, wound up and heaving the ball, and I said to the other guys, 'Hey, that looks like somebody I know,' and they said, 'A girl friend?' and I said, 'Heck no, my sister. That's my sister, Pete.'"

It was late, very late, when she went upstairs to her room. Her head was still whirling from the talk with Scott. It was always wonderful conversation when Scott came home. If she was closest to Hoyt, and respected Tim the most, and felt sorriest for Paul, and angriest at Bud, it was Scott whom she loved the most.

And all the stories he had to tell, the brilliant tales about rehearsals and theater people and stars he met on the way and how lonely and slightly sad many of the famous people were.

She set her toy heaver down on her desk and wound it up and once more watched it launch that perfect hook shot, over and over again. And she thought about the earlier part of the evening when she had felt so strange eating in that little restaurant with Burt Johnson. Not the Burt Johnson she had visualized as a child, but a quite different man. A man with feelings and some warmth, and the human compulsion to help another human being who needed help. And she realized why she had not told Scott or Mom, or even Gramp yet, who the new assistant coach at school was.

I need some quiet time to think about him, she told herself. I don't want to tell the family until I'm sure how I feel about him myself.

CHAPTER FIVE

Burt was waiting for her in the empty gym of Bamberger Hall when she pulled open the door and hurried into the place on Friday afternoon. He had brought a couple of thermos bottles and a bag of food in addition to the duffel bag of basketballs.

"I thought you might be hungry," he said. "There's Coke in one jug and milk in the other. And sandwiches in the bag."

"Hold the sandwiches till later. But I am thirsty." She poured out a cupful of Coke. "The caf at school had tuna casserole, and that makes me drink all afternoon."

He let her take her time. When she finished her drink, he said, "Pete, I'd better do some explaining, so you won't get all shook up."

"Shook up? What about?"

"About the way we're going to tackle this problem. I'll give it to you straight. We're going to teach you how to play basketball from scratch."

"You mean start from the beginning, with the fundamentals?"

"That's exactly what I mean."

"Whatever for? I've been playing since I was six. My brothers shoved a ball in my hand as soon as I could hold on to it."

"That may be the trouble."

"What do you mean?"

"If my theory works, I'll explain later. If it

doesn't, we'd accomplish nothing by discussing it."

The afternoon seemed a total waste of time no matter how she looked at it. Burt put her through such fundamentals as handling the ball involving the use of finger rather than palm control, something she had learned when she was eight.

"You have to imagine that there's wet paint on the ball," he shouted. "And keep those elbows close to your body." Again and again he called, "Stay thin, Pete!"

Dribbling also came in for its share of attention. He insisted that she wear a special pair of glasses he had brought. The lenses were taped across the lower part so she could see only through narrow slits across the top.

"That will keep you from watching the ball as you dribble," Burt explained.

She practiced low dribble with head and shoulders crouched down. High dribble with head and shoulders bent slightly forward. Dribbling with the right hand, the left hand, behind, to the side. "When can I take off these silly glasses?" she asked him.

"Right now. We'll start working on the pivot." They worked on the pivot until the balls of her feet were sore!

Fakes and feints were next. "Use everything," he told her. "Feet, hands, shoulders. And most important, use your eyes. The idea is to fool your opponent into thinking you'll do one thing when you intend to do another." Pete thought, As if I didn't know! Burt went on, "A player who can fake effectively is an excellent offensive threat. But don't overfake. That's amateurish and it wastes your strength. You have a tendency to fake too much with the ball and not enough with your body."

Next he drilled her in the rocker step, the fake shot and drive, the fake pass-off, the cross-over stop. Finally, he put her through drills for body balance and footwork, for improved stance, the whole gamut of passes from the two-handed chest pass on through the bounce and the over-head, the underhand, the sidearm, and the base-ball, up to the hook pass.

"The hook pass is a great help in getting a cornered player out of a bad spot," he explained. She thought, Tell me something I haven't heard before. But she kept still and did as he directed. At last he called a halt.

"No shooting?"

"Maybe next time, if we're ready for it."

"Whew, I'm bushed. Maybe I could go for that sandwich." He opened the paper bag and held it out. "Are you going to tell me your theory about what's wrong with my game?"

"No."

"Why not?"

"I said I'd wait until I was sure."

"You're a guy who sticks persistently to his word."

"I try to be honest."

"You've been honest to a fault with me," she said. She gave him a quizzical look. "And help-ful. And patient. In fact, you seem like a real friendly guy. Quite different from the trouble-maker who used to keep Bamberger Village jumping with rumbles. You've changed. Except that there still is that air of excitement wherever you are, even in basketball practices." She stopped, flushed, turning away as she realized that she had said more than she intended. She covered her embarrassment by asking, "What happened to change you?"

"Shakespeare called it 'the slings and arrows of outrageous fortune.' I call it the school of experience."

"You played pro basketball for a few years, didn't you?"

"Yes."

"I used to read about you and hear your name mentioned on the sports news, and sometimes I watched you play on television. You were a big name for a while, an important celebrity. You were going great guns. Then it stopped short. What happened?"

"Too much too soon, maybe. It never was any fun. The hours were terrible. You ate supper at two in the morning. You were bone-tired constantly, dreading having to get out of bed and go to the game. Pro sports aren't always filled with 'the milk of human kindness.' "

She grinned. "You're quoting Shakespeare again. You must have read his stuff."

"Right. I read a battered old volume on a round-the-world trip on a freighter and discovered that Will reads a lot better on the seven seas than he does in the schoolroom."

"Keep telling me about your thing with the pros."

"Like I said, it was punishment. You look at your opponents and you think you see fangs. You feel they're out to get you. And inside yourself is this bitter hostility too. You have to be equipped with what they call killer instinct to get through some of those games, especially if you want to win, and who doesn't. I got so I wasn't proud of my own attitudes and feelings. A thing like that can wear you down. When you have to live with it week after week, you want to run away — somewhere, anywhere, just so long as you never heft a basketball again."

"That's how I felt toward the end of the Southport game."

"Yes, I realized you did." He put the sandwiches away. "Don't eat too much. I thought we'd pick up a snack again somewhere and talk some more."

She backed away, suddenly tense and uneasy. "I have a date. A boy I know is playing with the Bradford team and afterward there's a dance. He's asked me to the game and the dance. And Connie Anderson and her friend Bill are going too." In her nervousness she blatted out more than she meant to tell him.

"What about getting together tomorrow?"

"Saturdays I help this friend with his basketball game, like you're helping me. I know it sounds strange, me needing help and having the nerve to help someone else. He's a good athlete but new at basketball, and his team needs his support. So he likes to practice with me. I mean, he wants to put in as much practice as he can."

"Shawn Patrick?"

"How did you guess?"

"No guess. Everyone knows about Shawn. He's pulled Bradford right up out of the dumps. I'm sure he makes a good friend too. Will you spend the whole day with him tomorrow?"

"No," she said quickly. "After lunch Connie and I go shopping and then I spend some time with Gramp. You remember Gramp O'Hara."

"I ought to! He kicked me out of your yard so many times I lost count. He said I didn't have sufficient compassion to be a good human being and that he hoped life would teach me a few lessons. It has. Gramp O'Hara was right."

"I ought to be going, honestly. I have to eat and change my clothes. Connie's picking me up around seven so we can get good seats for the game."

"When I asked about tomorrow, Pete, I didn't mean what you were doing during the day. I'd like to take you out in the evening. Supper somewhere and afterward whatever you like. There are places to dance. Or a movie."

"I can't. Honestly, I can't." She backed toward the door, gathering up her things, her coat, shoulder bag. "I've already got something to do in the evening too. Connie and I have tickets for the dance at Toth Hall. They always put on a great dance there and —" She interrupted herself, embarrassed by her nervous volubility. "Thanks for the invitation, anyway. I'd better hurry along. See you."

She had left the Porsche at home, knowing that the parking area around Bamberger Hall would not be cleared. Now she ran all the way, running as if her life depended upon it. Running away from Burt Johnson. Why? she asked herself. Why?

When she went through the back door into the kitchen, she found a note from her mother on the counter.

"Dear Pete, Paul wants me to go out to an early supper with him. He does need cheering up. Supper's fixed and in the frig. All you have to do is to heat it. There's a surprise upstairs in your room. I hope you like it. Go over and show Gramp. It will make him feel good. Have a wonderful time. Love, M. P.S. I'm wearing my wool cape, so why don't you borrow my fake fur coat for tonight, Pete? When you tried it on, it looked great."

Pete put her supper in the oven and ran upstairs. The door of her room was ajar. She could see the "surprise" hanging on an old-fashioned clothes tree.

"It's a new dress!" she exclaimed to the empty hallway. "Mom went and bought me a new dress for the dance!" She hurried in and had a look. She had asked Shawn what to wear and he had told her that some of the girls would probably wear pants, but that since she was asking, he would like to see her in a dress.

Yesterday she had complained out loud that she had a couple of skirts and plenty of sweaters but no suitable dresses that fit anymore.

She stood there looking at her new dress. It was a dark-blue velveteen shirtwaist style. She took a quick shower and got into the dress. It fit perfectly.

Pete went into her mother's room where there was a full-length mirror and had a look at herself.

"This is really me?" she exclaimed. "Oh, wow, will Shawn Patrick be surprised!" She turned around several times and examined her profile and derriere. "It looks great," she said to her reflection. "Now all I have to do is put in some time matching up the rest of the equipment to the dress."

She fussed with her hair, trying to do with it what Connie had done the other day down in the girls' locker room, swirling the bangs across her forehead and giving the ends a flip to make a softer frame for her face. "It's not as expert as Connie's demonstration," she told herself, "but it's a lot better than my usual gone-with-the-wind effect." She studied her face. She didn't have the makeup paraphernalia, eye stuff and all that. She fished in her drawer and came up with three chewed-off lipsticks that were as dry as they could be. Then she remembered that Mom kept a special "kit" of extras in a drawer in the downstairs bathroom.

She ran downstairs, found the kit, and helped herself to a brand-new lipstick. When it took three or four tries before she got it on to suit her, she commented, "The first hundred years of using this stuff must be the hardest."

Suddenly she remembered that she had not eaten. "I'll have to do the whole blame thing over again," she wailed.

As she was stacking the dishes, she heard the horn of Bill's car. She snatched up her mother's coat and shrugged into it. When she ran out to the car, Connie whistled, "Wow, look at the glamour gal. Hey, Pete, you look great."

She poked her head in. "Smell. I even swiped some perfume for the occasion. And I've got a new dress. Mom bought it for me. She wants Gramp to see me, and I ought to say good night to him. Could you wait a few minutes? Or maybe you'd like to run over to Gramp's with me."

"We'd better wait. If we all descend on him,

we'll never get away. He'll want to serve refreshments and talk."

"Right you are. I'll hurry it."

She had to bang so loud that she guessed he must have fallen asleep over a book. He opened the door, rubbing his eyes. "Pete. Come on in."

"I can't stay, Gramp. This is a quickie. Mom wanted me to show you." She threw off her coat and waltzed around for him. "How do you like it?"

"It's magnificent, that it certainly is. Where are you heading?"

"To the basketball game at Bradford High, to see Shawn play, and a dance afterward. If I had time, you and I would have ourselves a waltz before I left." She kissed him on the cheek. "Now you're full of my brand-new lipstick which I scrounged from Mom's special supply. So, wish me a good time and go wash your face."

"That I do, Pete. The best ever." He stood in the doorway, waving good-by as she crossed over to Bill's car and they drove off.

The game was an exciting one, and close. Bradford and New Cornwall were evenly matched. Both playing the Big D, a strong defensive game. Bradford won and Pete was glad, for Shawn's sake. But what interested her most was her observation of Shawn in action, within the framework of a major game. Tonight, for the first time, she had the opportunity to see Shawn's style, its strong points and its flaws. She made notes throughout the quarters, labeling them, in her mind, "To be discussed during our practice sessions."

Shawn waited for them before going down to the shower room. "Look, there's a table reserved for us in the other gym. Ross Plummer, the chairman of the dance committee, is a good friend of mine. I told him about our group and he said not to worry, he'd take care of you."

Bradford's "second gym" had been given a nightclub atmosphere for the occasion, with tables arranged around the dance floor. Pete was impressed. The theme of the dance was "A Day in Montmartre" and the committee had done a good job, giving an arty, if not apache, look to the place. Posters of the Impressionist painters were tacked up on the walls. The tablecloths were red-and-white checked, the lights were discreetly dim and the committee flitted about garbed in turn-of-the-century costumes that looked really Parisian.

By the time Shawn joined them, the band was in full swing and the dance floor was crowded. Ross Plummer asked Pete if she wanted to dance, but she said no, she guessed she would wait and have the first one with Shawn. She saw him coming across the room wending his way between the tables, stopping now and then to accept the congratulations of his classmates and friends. She knew how he felt. She had been there herself. But Shawn came more naturally by it. He seemed to revel in it. She had noticed this exuberance while the game was on. That high note of involvement which Shawn had been able to hold throughout the game. This was something new to her. She lived for basketball and if anyone had asked her, she would have said she loved it, but she did not get the big kick out of it that Shawn did. She was a better hoopster than he was or ever would be — when she was at her best and didn't have a wrist problem — but the responsibility of the game weighed heavily on her.

"Hi," he said, pulling out a chair. "Let's sit a minute till I get my second wind. Okay?"

"You bet. This is great, Shawn. I mean, the atmosphere. We don't do things like this over at Central."

"I thought you might like it." He was studying her. "You look wonderful tonight, Pete. I like your dress."

"Mom bought it for me. This afternoon. I didn't have a decent dress to wear and I guess she felt sorry for me." She stopped, realizing that she had said the wrong thing. She grinned. "Shawn, how do you stand me? You pay me a compliment, and I have to go into a song and dance that spoils the whole thing. Do you suppose I'll ever learn?"

He put his hand over hers. "I like you the way you are. Remember?" His hand touched Pete's, but she watched his eyes. They were roving. Across the dance floor. Pete herself had seen Susan Alpert long ago, the moment she had sat down at the table. She could not have avoided seeing Susan, because Susan was the first girl out on the dance floor. Her partner was a tall boy, handsome in a rugged way, with a certain tough hardness to his features. Pete guessed he was a football player. But for all the guy's good looks, it was Susan Alpert you had to keep your eyes on. She was that kind of girl. Now Pete could understand why Shawn had said, I'd like to see you in a dress. Some of the girls did wear pants, but Susan Alpert was wearing a dress. Not just any dress, but *the* dress — the most outstanding dress on the dance floor. Simple elegance was the phrase for it, all line and fabric and color. A rich shade of turquoise that turned every male head on the floor. Shawn could not take his eyes off her, or if he could, he didn't.

"I think she's stunning too," Pete said.

He turned, startled to be caught Susan-watching. "Let's dance," he said. "The music is too good to waste on small talk." Pete noticed that even when they went out on the floor, he kept looking toward Susan Alpert. And Susan looked at Shawn. And smiled. And raised her free hand ever so slightly, just enough, to signal to Shawn that she knew he was there and that he was watching.

Shawn danced with Susan. One dance. It was Pete who prompted him. "I think you should, Shawn. It's right and she expects it. You know what you said, she's a good friend."

"Okay, if you insist, Pete. I'll bring over the guy she's with and introduce him so you can have this dance with him."

"No, Shawn," Pete stopped him. "I'd like to watch. There's a lot to see here tonight."

She went up the stairs to the small balcony and stood there alone, looking down and watching them. She felt a strange sudden insecurity. The girl was so right for Shawn, so perfect. Pete had seen her on the basketball court and thought her a fine athlete. Pete had admired her style, her game. But this was a different Susan Alpert. This was a woman, not a girl. Everything about her was outstanding. Not just her clothes, although they were a big part of the impression she made. There were other things, not just face and hair, but extras. The way she held her head, the way she carried herself, the swift small gesture she would make, the laughter that Pete could not hear but knew was there by the way Susan leaned back and looked up at Shawn. Her talk would be perfect too. The right subject matter, the right words, and diction, and tone.

Not like Pete. Spoiling his compliment about her dress by that silly chitchat about needing a dress for the occasion and her mother buying it for her, as if it mattered, as if Shawn would care. Naïve, that's what Pete told herself she was. Naïve and unseasoned. Green. A greener, Gramp would have that name for it. Someone who did not know anything about anything. She could not even pick out her own clothes. She'd rather have her sisters-in-law or her mother buy things for her. Her friend Connie had to show her how to do her hair. And she did not even own a usable lipstick. Or perfume. Or a decent coat.

She looked down at Shawn and Susan again.

I'll change, she told herself. I'm going to be different from now on. I would like to look like Susan Alpert. To act and talk and carry myself like her. I can't, of course. I can never be Susan Alpert. But maybe, just maybe, I can be a different me.

CHAPTER SIX

She called Connie before breakfast the next morning.

"Hi, this is Pete."

"For Pete's sake, Pete, it's not even eight o'clock. I was fast asleep."

"I know. Last night was fun, yes?"

"Sure it was. The dance was great. Bill said thanks. Did you get home all right? Did Shawn want to neck?"

"Oh, shut up!"

"Well, did he?"

"Connie, I'm calling because I want to know how I can get an appointment with Francesca."

"You what? Hey, Pete, I don't think I heard right. You want to what?"

"You heard me. I have to meet Shawn at the canteen by nine and we're going through a shooting session. But this afternoon I want to have my hair done. That's the way you say it, isn't it?"

"It's the way you say it, all right. Pete, are you feeling well?"

"Never felt better in my life."

"For a few seconds I thought you were whacked out of your wig, talking about going to a hairdresser. I thought you were serious."

"Connie, I mean it. I want my hair done."

"Wow, I'll have to call and see what I can do. Saturdays are busy, but Francesca is related by marriage and she'll do anything for the family. What do you want done, Pete?"

"Whatever I can get for five bucks that will make me look half as good as Susan Alpert."

"Pete, you're a nut." Connie laughed. "I'll bet it's on account of Shawn that you're doing this. You're in love, aren't you?"

"Nope."

"When a girl starts to remake herself, its got to be because of a man."

"Not this gal, Connie. You try to get that appointment for me. I'll call you from the canteen to see how you made out."

When Pete joined Shawn in the gym at the canteen, the first thing he said was, "I saw you making notes last night at the game. Did you bring them along?"

She pulled the slip of paper from her pocket but kept a tight grip on it. "Maybe I should mind my own business."

"Why? If you saw things wrong with my game, it's better to hear about my weaknesses from a friend."

"It's not a question of weaknesses. You're building a strong game defensively. You spark the team's action. I never saw Bradford so steamed up about basketball. Or working so well together."

"You're stalling because you're got something down on that paper that you're afraid to mention."

"I'm trying to figure how to say it without losing a friend."

"Just spill it. Don't turn tactful and spoil your public image."

"Well, it's this. I think you're making a mistake trying to concentrate on the spectacular center-court shots, Shawn. I don't like to sound

68

square, but the truth is that you practically have to be born with a basketball on your fist to do the kind of stuff you're spending your energy on. You're wearing yourself out on grandstand plays when you could conserve your strength and accomplish more with simpler stuff."

"Are you suggesting I become a pivot man?"

"Pivot man! Don't be ridiculous. What I really want to say is that with some practice you could become a terrific bucket player."

"You mean a guy who plays within his own free-throw lane or close to it, a guy whose prime function is to pass off to a teammate?"

"No, definitely not. That's old-fashioned. That's not the kind of bucket player I mean. There are great pro bucket players who do some mighty important shooting. Of course, you've got to have the nerve for it."

"What do you mean, the nerve for it?"

"You've got to have the nerve to start with your back to the basket, which is breaking the primary rule of shooting to begin with. Then you run the risk of a box defense from the Big D when they catch on to your strategy, which is to pivot and toss the ball through the hoop right there in your own free-throw lane as often as you can get your hands on it."

"The rule book says you can stay in your own free-throw lane not more than three seconds while the ball is in play and controlled by your team. So it has to be one heck of a quick shot."

"Okay. So you need speed as well as nerve. Why don't we concentrate on that today — on developing speed? It's the one thing I know something about. Because I grew up playing basketball with boys, my brothers. And if you don't think that develops speed in a female, you can guess again. I had to learn all the angles or I would have been lost in the shuffle."

"Sure, let's give it a try."

They spent the entire morning on the bucket play. Shawn caught on to it even more quickly than she had expected he would.

"See," she told him, "you've got the stuff for it. A few more days practicing and you'll be perfect. If I were you, I wouldn't let on to anyone, not even your teammates, that you're concentrating on the bucket shot. Word gets around too fast. Spring it as a surprise tactic in your next game."

Around ten thirty she checked with Connie on the public phone in the foyer.

"You've got an appointment," Connie told her. "A late one. Francesca is staying overtime because you're a friend of mine. She's giving you a styling as well as a shampoo and color rinse, but you're not to tell anyone. The price is not only special, Pete, it's phenomenal."

Around twelve thirty Shawn suggested they quit and run over to the Friendly for lunch. After they had eaten, he asked her if she'd like to take a ride out into the country. She said yes, so long as she got back by four. It was a good afternoon. The back roads were cleared and although the weather prediction had been for light snow, it had not yet begun to fall. When they reached the meadowy stretch beyond the old reservoir, Shawn pulled into a picnic area.

"I've got a couple of pairs of snowshoes in the trunk," he said. "Left over from my last boarding school, which was high up in snow country. Game for a hike?"

"Sure, why not?" It was fun. She had never used snowshoes before and at first they felt clumsy and strange, but she soon got used to them. They trekked for half a mile before Shawn pulled a small camera from one of his pockets, and said, "Lean against that tree, Pete. I want some pictures of you."

"I'm not photogenic," she called to him. "I'd rather go to the dentist than have my picture taken, but I'll oblige if you'll let me take yours. And give me one."

"It's a deal."

Shawn took a dozen or more of Pete and then let her snap a few of him.

When they got back to the car, she stood by and watched Shawn stow away the snowshoes. He closed the car trunk and turned around, pulling her toward him.

"There's a great song entitled 'Put Your Head on My Shoulder.' "

"I guess I can take a hint." She snuggled against his parka. She shivered. "Brr, that's a cold resting place."

"It will be warmer in the car." He opened the door for her. They sat, not talking, for a long time. It was Shawn who broke the silence. "How do you feel about going steady with a guy, Pete?"

"I've never even *gone* with a guy before, no less thought about the steady business! What are you getting at, Shawn?"

"Let's go steady, Pete."

"What does that mean?"

"That we don't date anyone else and see each other a lot."

"What about Susan?"

"Susan's engaged. That was Rod Cushman

with her last night. He's a college junior and serious about Susan. She was wearing a ring with a blue stone, I think she called it an aquamarine, that he gave her. She doesn't like diamonds. They're too cold."

For the first time, she felt angry with Shawn. Charm or no charm, she was going to speak her mind.

"I don't think you want to go steady, Shawn. I think you want somebody to soothe your ego."

"Now why do you say that, Pete?"

"Because I think it's true. You're a little like the fellow who goes in on election day and says to himself, I'm not actually voting for the candidate I've chosen, I'm voting against the other guy. You're on the rebound, Shawn."

"Don't be ridiculous. I told you Susan and I were just friends."

"Maybe you cared for her more than you thought you did. You have a special way of looking at her, Shawn. Last night I went up on the balcony and watched you dance with her. You looked right together, a perfect couple."

"I told you I'm crazy about you, Pete. I can't get you out of my mind. I wouldn't lie about a thing like that."

"Maybe you have thought about me a lot. After all, I'm here, and we like the same things, and enjoy being together. Yes, I think you do like me a lot, Shawn; but to go steady is to make a commitment, and people shouldn't do that unless they are involved with each other. Not superficially but deeply."

"Is that your answer?"

"For now, yes."

"Maybe we shouldn't see each other at all if that's the way you feel. If you don't trust me enough and trust what I've told you about my feelings to go along with me, maybe we should cool it."

"That's up to you, Shawn. You call the signals."

He started the car and, turning in a wide arc, swung out of the picnic area. It was a long, cold, silent ride back to Bamberger Village.

CHAPTER SEVEN

Toth Hall was no country club, Pete had to admit. But in terms of decor and atmosphere, it was the most attractive of the recreation centers that "graced" Bamberger Village. The Hungarians had a way with color. The floors were carpeted in a rich maroon. There were gold-colored curtains at the windows and touches of gold and red in the upholstery, the lamps, the wallpaper.

Pete and Connie had been late, arriving when the dance downstairs was already in full swing, so they now had the powder room to themselves. Pete took a look at herself in the gilt-framed mirror as she waited for Connie to finish retying her scarf. Pete found it hard to believe that she was staring at her own image. It was not just the restyling which softened her face, giving it a more feminine expression. It was the color! "I'm going to give you a lightening rinse," Francesca had told her. "No extra charge." And Pete, not understanding exactly what that meant, had made no protests. Now she saw! From a drab, light-brown, nondescript thatch, her hair had miraculously become what Francesca had dubbed "Champagne."

"It's not me," she said out loud to the mirror.

Connie turned. "What's not you?"

"That kookie blond color."

"Your hair gets real light in summer, Pete."

"That's different. It gets crazy in summer, ten

different shades, some light, some darker, and everyone knows it's on account of the sun and salt water. This isn't natural."

"I think you look great."

"I think I look terrible. So does Mom. And Gramp too."

"Did they say so?"

"It's what they *didn't* say that counts. When they like something, they tell me. When they stare at me for five whole minutes and then say something about the weather instead of my hair, it means they are giving me the thumbs-down of silence. In our family that is the most effective disapproval you can get."

"Let's see what my Bill has to say about it. He's coming to the dance after he closes up shop. Bill has taste."

Pete didn't want to argue the point. "There goes the young people's band blasting off with a rock czardas," she said. "We better go down."

Connie was still fussing with her scarf when they entered the "ballroom." It was a large rectangular room with a bandstand at each end. On one of the platforms was a gypsy orchestra, mostly violins, the older men dressed in flamboyant continental style. On the other, was the young people's band. They had given themselves the name of Rhapsody in Rock.

There was always a sizable bunch of singles at the Saturday dances in Toth Hall. Someone called from the crowd, "Hey, Pete, what have you done to your hair?" Some laughter followed. Pete was glad when a couple of boys separated themselves from the group and asked Connie and her to dance.

Pete's partner was Bela Georgy, a boy who lived on the cliffs of Bamberger Village where the Magyars of several generations ago had built their houses. Bela had the Magyar look, tall, intense, fiery dark eyes, bright colors in his cheeks. A gypsy look. He danced as most Magyars did — with dedication. So much so, that Pete had to concentrate — really stay with it — to keep up with him.

As they passed the onlookers, a voice called, "Hi, Georgy, who's that with you? *Celery Top?*" And another voice chimed in, "Say, that's a good nickname for Pete. *Celery Top.*"

Bela steered her toward the other side of the dance floor.

"I'm sorry," he said. "There's got to be one of them in every crowd. Don't let it throw you, Pete."

"It won't. I'm used to worse than that on the basketball court." Just the same it bothered her, especially because she blamed herself for letting Francesca lighten her hair. She was glad that Bela stayed near the doors and avoided the lineup along the wall.

Pete was not sure exactly when she became aware that someone was standing in the doorway and staring at her. She looked over Bela's shoulder and saw Burt Johnson. Burt was not smiling, just looking. She felt that rush of feeling which always swept over her when Burt was close by. Tonight he looked more handsome than ever, dressed as if he had just come in from the great outdoors instead of for a dance at Toth Hall. His corduroy pants were of a deep taupe, the same shade as the suede vest that hung loosely over a pale bulky knit turtleneck sweater.

"Hi, Burt," she called.

The next moment he cut in, clapping Bela on the shoulder and giving him a slight shove.

Bela was left alone, gaping his surprise as Burt whisked Pete away. She shook her head. "That was rude. Not even a word to Bela. You should have asked. It wasn't a nice thing to do."

"It would have been less nice if I had said what I was thinking."

"I'm afraid to ask."

"This woman is mine."

"That's not the truth."

"It's truth enough for me. I only came here tonight so I could be with you."

"I shouldn't have told you what Connie and I were planning to do."

"I'd have found out anyway."

"How could you?"

"I have ways and means. I don't give my secrets away."

He danced well, but then most natural athletes did. She told him so. "You're a good dancer."

"So are you."

Throughout the evening, he never left her side. Several times she said, "I ought to dance with some of the others. They expect it. Especially Bela Georgy — you were so rude to him."

"You've been dancing with them for years. This is the first time you've danced with me."

"You're possessive and selfish."

"Sure I am. When I care about someone, I want to be with that person. Don't you?"

"I don't know," she answered. "There are a lot of things I'm not sure about anymore. You're sure about everything. I guess that's what you call strength."

Around eleven he said, "Isn't that Connie's friend who just came in?"

"Yes. Bill Rollins."

"Then you won't have to wait and go home with her."

"No, but I should. Usually we team up with one of the boys, Bela or Ernie or Steve, to make a foursome for a late snack. You want to join us, Burt?"

"No, I want you for myself without Connie and her boyfriend." He smiled. "You said I was selfish."

"It's time for the Lucky Number dance. We ought to wait."

"No, let's go now. This place gets hectic just before midnight."

He was right about that. The Magyar enthusiasm gained momentum as the evening drew to a close.

"Go get your coat," he told her. "I left my jacket in the car, parked close to the side door. I'll meet you there."

"Where are we going?"

"You'll see when we get there."

He drove out toward Rockwood, a long ride over back-country roads until he turned at last toward the shore and followed a narrow lane that wound up and up toward a high ridge. He seemed to be familiar with the place and to know exactly where to find a clearing to park. When he pulled over, he asked her, "Could you stand a short walk?"

"I guess so. It's not so cold," she answered. "It's warming up to snow."

"It won't snow till morning."

"How do you know?"

"I have a feeling about things like that: the sea, the stars, the sky, the snow, the rain. There's a path cleared for walking. This place has a watchman. He lives up there, in that house on the cliff. He's become a friend of mine, because I come here so often. Come on, I want you to see something."

Burt held her hand, leading her up a steplike incline. When they reached the top of the ridge, he took her by the shoulders and turned her around. A railing ran around the knoll on which they stood. She looked down and drew in her breath sharply, a gasp of surprise.

Below was the sea, churning against the rocks. A high cold moon lighted the dark waters.

"Why, it's beautiful! I didn't know the sea was this close."

"Few people do." He put his arm around her, holding her close. "That's to keep you warm," he told her.

"What is this place?"

"A Marine lookout, connected with the Coast Guard. That's what it is nowadays."

"What did it used to be?"

"A few hundred years ago it was an Indian meeting place."

"Then there must be a legend."

"Fifty of them. The one I like best hasn't yet been told."

"I'm supposed to ask what it is."

"Someday I'll tell you. At the right time."

"You have a special talent for promising to tell things later on, at the right time. First, your theory about my shooting problem, and now this. Why did you want me to see this place?"

"Because, as you agreed, it's beautiful and I

wanted to share it. Things that are beautiful are no good experienced alone. They need sharing or you lose them. Come on, I don't want you to get chilled. We'll go back to the car."

When they climbed into the car, he pulled a blanket from the rear, threw it over her lap and pulled her close. He didn't make any attempt to kiss her quickly as Shawn had done, and she was glad of that. She needed time to get used to him, to the excitement of his nearness.

"Can you stand a bit of conversation?" he asked.

"Sure, I'm a talker myself."

"Well, I'm not especially. Not a talker, that is. But I want to talk about you, about why you are running away from me."

"Running away? Yes, I suppose that's true. I am."

"Why?"

"You're a teacher, for one thing."

"Not yet, not for a couple of years."

"A coach, then. And to me it's the same thing. I could never feel right dating a teacher. I know it has happened sometimes. Young teachers, male or female, being close to their students in age. Close in other ways, seeing each other every day, things in common. They go out, and I know about a few that got engaged and married. I can't see it. There has to be a line somewhere."

"That's not the reason you're running away."

She turned away, looking out of the window into the moon shadows of the bushes.

"Is it because I'm part Indian?"

She swung sharply around. "Of course not. In Bamberger Village everyone is part something. Me, I'm a United Nations. I have so many nationalities in my background I can blame a different one for every fault I have. Besides, American Indian is something to be proud that you are."

"Then is it because of my earlier notoriety?" He was teasing. She could see the faint smile in the dark. "Seriously, I know what I was and the stories that went around. I was a wild, crazy kid."

"That's past and you've changed. No one can hold what a person used to be against him when he's changed so much."

He reached out in the darkness and stroked her cheek. "Tell me what it is, Pete. Why are you running?"

"Okay, so you want to know. You're asking. You make me feel afraid."

"Afraid? Why? How?"

"I don't know. I honestly don't know. Only when I'm close to you. Not on the basketball court, that's different. But other times, like this, or when we're just sitting alone talking, I don't know what it is, but I feel like I want to run away."

"Pete, I think I'm beginning to understand. It's not me you're running from. It's yourself. You're in love."

"In love! Me, in love? Not on your life."

"Are you sure?"

The question threw her. She wasn't sure, not of anything.

"If I wanted to think about love, there's Shawn Patrick. This afternoon he asked me to go steady."

"And what did you tell him?"

She remembered how angry she had been with Shawn and she blurted out the truth heatedly. "I told him it was a nutty idea. That he ought to have more sense than to think I'd take him on the rebound just because Susan Alpert went and got herself engaged to some college junior with enough dough to buy her a ring. An aquamarine. Not a diamond, diamonds are too cold for the high-and-mighty Susan." She paused and looked at Burt. "See what I mean, I've done it again. Opened my big mouth."

"That's why you changed your hair, on account of Susan."

"No! Yes, to be truthful, yes, I did. Last night at the dance, I insisted Shawn dance with her and I watched them from up on the balcony, and they looked so right together, and Susan was so perfect, and I decided to change myself. A new me."

"You shouldn't have done that."

"You don't like my hair?"

"I didn't mean that. I meant you shouldn't have decided to change yourself on account of another girl."

"I asked you if you liked my hair this way."

"There's nothing wrong with it. The style and the color are fine. It's just not you. Tonight when I saw you dancing with Bela Georgy, I thought at first that it was another girl. I liked you the way you were. All windblown and casual and a little bit sloppy. No makeup. Face shining out on a tough, hard-boiled mean old world, saying, 'Hey, guys, things aren't so bad after all. There's real joy to be had, some fun and maybe a bit of happiness. Climb on the bandwagon, and let's go for broke.' That was you. That's the girl I like."

She sat quietly beside him for a few moments.

"It's getting cold," she said. "And I'm hungry. I get hungry when I dance a lot."

"We'll find a place." He turned on the ignition, but before he started the car she reached and put her hand over his.

"You're right about a lot of things, Burt. I hate to admit it, but you are. Maybe I have been running away from myself. And about the hair, don't think I'm sore because you don't like it. Let's call it an idea that bombed. I'm going to wash the color out as fast as I can fill the basin with water, or the kids will have a new name for me. Celery Top!"

CHAPTER EIGHT

The next couple of weeks went by in a whirl for Pete. She lost track of the days. It seemed as if she was on the basketball court most of her waking hours. Central High played three more games. New Cornwall traveled to Central High for a game that Pete's team won by a narrow margin, 55-52. The game with Elmhurst at Elmhurst was also a close one, but Central High managed a final five-point lead with a score of 47-42. At Beecham, Central High won a decisive victory, swamping Beecham 60-22.

Although her team was racking up points toward a county championship, Pete had personal problems in every game.

In the game with New Cornwall, she had an unprecedented spree of fouling. The first two fouls were for "charging," when, overeager to make a goal, she whammed into the guards who were legally defending the basket. The third foul was called on her for "pushing" while she was trying to get into position for a rebound under the basket. Then, upset by her record, Pete hit the jackpot when she attempted to stop a pass and inadvertently hacked two of the New Cornwall forwards bringing a blast from the PA system: "Multiple foul on Phillips. Pete Phillips is disqualified with five fouls."

At Elmhurst she ran into trouble from the stands. The spectators were against her because Burt Johnson had given Pete a tough assignment in man-to-man defense for the Elmhurst game. Elmhurst was a school with intense competitive spirit. This year they had only one — ONE — outstanding shooter. Aggie Harrison. In the man-to-man strategy, Burt had assigned Pete to battle it out with Aggie. It was to Pete's credit that she had rallied from her clumsiness of the New Cornwall game and did a more than adequate job of blocking the Elmhurst bombshell, Aggie Harrison, without having any personal fouls called on her. But the spectators who were rooting for Elmhurst were outraged. They heckled Pete throughout the game. It cramped her style at the basket. The old wrist trouble plagued her and she missed everything but easy crip shots.

In the game with Beecham, Pete's wrist acted up in earnest. She couldn't understand why. The game was an easy win. The Beecham stands were far from filled, and the crowd was lethargic toward its own team. There was none of the heckling or the razzmatazz of a big night game. Yet there it was, that crazy twist in her wrist, again and again.

Fortunately the rest of the girls had profited from Burt Johnson's coaching. Central High came through, in spite of a handicapped ace shooter, with three sure victories that kept the team in the running for the championship.

"No thanks to me," Pete commented wryly to Connie. "If it hadn't been for what Burt's been able to do with the speed, style, and shooting of the rest of the team, we'd have lost those three games."

"Don't blame yourself," Connie consoled Pete. "We all have our low periods."

"How low can you get?" Pete wanted to know.

Pete expected Burt to call her on the mat for a lecture after each game. He did no such thing. His only comment was, "Be sure you show up for our extra practice sessions." Once she asked him, "Aren't you going to bawl me out for the way I've been playing, or rather the way I *haven't* been shooting?"

"Why should I?" he asked.

"It would make me feel less guilty if you scolded a little."

"You don't scold a wounded animal," he said. "You mend it." For once she knew enough to keep her mouth closed and not respond with some flip retort.

The team was practicing almost every afternoon on which no game was scheduled, so Burt had arranged for evening sessions with Pete. A few adult clubs and lodges had their headquarters in Bamberger Hall, using the small conference rooms. This gave Pete and Burt some company, but they did have the barnlike gymnasium to themselves.

Every evening, like clockwork, Pete would rush in to find Burt already there, banging the ball against the backboard for a perfect banked shot or dribbling out for a spectacular, two-handed overhead which never missed. He would turn and say, "Hi, Pete, glad you made it early. Let's see how my superstar shooter is doing tonight."

It was a joke between them because of that crack she had made when he had asked her to play pivot during his first coaching session with the girls' team. And it was especially funny since so far he had given her no extra help whatsoever with her shooting!

For the first week, Burt continued to drill Pete on what she considered elementary skills. Not once did he devote any specific time to basket-shooting. Each night, at the end of the practice, she would throw him a knowing grin and ask, "When do we start shooting?"

She knew what the answer would be: "When we're ready."

It got so she did not mind his coaching methods, unorthodox though they had appeared to be at the beginning. In fact, she began to see what she called "the light at the end of the tunnel." Subtly at first, and then more obviously, she recognized the improvements that were being made in her style. A little awkwardness here, minor flaws there — these were being eliminated. Her recoil was better on the catch as she received a pass. Her ball-handling had definitely improved. So had her pivoting, her stance, her finger control of the ball, her balance, and her footwork.

But most of all, she was learning the art of timing.

Burt talked about this so much that at first she tuned him out, thinking that he was merely harping on a favorite subject. But as the week progressed, she realized that she had better listen and listen well, that this was perhaps the most important single factor in the difference between a good basketball player and a great one.

Burt delivered a regular lecture on the subject.

"Ever watch the old silent movies on television?" he asked. "The old comedians, for instance?"

"Not too often."

"Then find a channel that has the shows and watch them. The old boys were masters of timing. They weren't afraid to take their time. An actor has to have it to be good, this ability to hesitate and take his time when he should. So must the athlete. You could have every other quality of a great athlete — strength, grace, physique, control — but if your timing is off, you'll never make the big leagues."

"I should think you'd have to be born with it!" she commented.

"That would help," Burt said with a smile, "but it can be learned too."

"How do I rate?"

"So far, fair to middling. You've got a certain natural sense for timing, but you abuse it. There's this something in your nature, an impatience, a fidgetiness that betrays your natural ability. Fear, too, can be the basis of poor timing. Fear makes a player push the panic button. The ability to be able to wait for the right moment to make a move in any situation — on-stage, in world affairs, in personal relationships — is the greatest asset a person can have."

"And on the basketball court too."

"And on the basketball court too," he nodded.

The evenings were not all work and lectures, however. There were the times in between and afterward. Sometimes Pete would bring over her dessert and a helping for Burt — a pastry, a piece of cake or pie her mother had baked. Burt would have a thermos bottle of coffee for himself and another of milk for Pete, and they would sit up on the old cafeteria-type table that had been pushed against the wall and relax and talk. Not about basketball, but about other things.

She learned a great deal about Burt Johnson.

"You've traveled a lot," she said to him one night. "What, in your opinion, is the most romantic spot in the world?"

He smiled at her. "I notice you said most *romantic*."

She flushed and looked away. "I meant interesting."

"I'll settle for your first choice," he told her. "Romantic. Let's see. Most people would say the South Seas, I suppose, and they are, of course, if you can find any unspoiled spot. But there are plenty of others. The Australian Outback presents a challenge all its own. In Europe there are the mountains, and Capri still has its fans, and parts of the Orient, mostly the parts that are almost impossible to get to. Every man has two things within his secret self that he dreams about."

Remembering Shawn's confession, she was curious about Burt's cherished dreams. She asked him, "What are they?"

"Every man has his Shangri-la and his Island."

"I'm not sure I dig."

"Shangri-la, a place that is unknown to the rest of the world, a paradise on earth where people are happy and kind to each other, where no one ever grows old or ill or lonely, where everything is beautiful."

"Is the Marine Watch out by the sea your Shangri-la?"

"Not really. Anything you ever reach could only be second-best to a real Shangri-la. To be genuine it could not exist, you see. Except in the private imagination."

"And what about the island?"

"I capitalize it — Island, with a capital 'I.' Every man dreams of owning one. His own, exclusively."

"Why? I should think it would be the loneliest spot on earth, and loneliness isn't good."

"It would never be lonely on a man's Island. There he can gather together all the exciting, adventurous, brilliant, interesting people in the world. People he reads about or hears about but never meets. And so the man who owns the Island is perpetually happy, entertained and *needed*. All the dreadful things that happen to ordinary human beings who do not own an Island cannot happen to this man. Things like boredom, irritation, pressure, pettiness, all the junk in the world. No place on the Island for any of it."

"Shawn has a different dream."

"What's that?"

"He dreams about meeting a certain kind of girl who would be comfortable to be with, sharing interests, a good listener, *simpático*. The perfect female, that's Shawn Patrick's dream — finding her."

Burt stared into Pete's eyes. "That too is Everyman's dream, Pete. Along with his Shangri-la and his Island."

She jumped down from her perch on the table and faced him, a broad grin on her face. "Last one to the basket has to pivot fifty times," she told him and ran lickety-split across the court.

One night she took him over to see Gramp. Unannounced. I have to do it that way, she told herself. Any other way would be disastrous. She told Burt why. "I want Gramp to know you now, the way you are today," she said. "He's got this picture of you as a hellion, the boy he kicked out of the Phillips backyard every chance he got. It's not going to be easy, Burt, introducing him to the Burt Johnson I've come to know. In fact, I've avoided talking much about you. I merely mentioned that we're getting in some extra practice with the basketball and that you are our bona fide coach. Do you think you can take it? Gramp can be a handful when he's feeling ornery or doesn't like someone."

"We'll give it a try," Burt agreed.

It was an evening that Pete would long remember. She equipped Burt and herself with ammunition, an anchovy pizza, which Gramp liked, and around eight thirty, after basketball practice, she banged on the cottage door. When Gramp opened it, Pete said, "I've got one thing you like, an anchovy pizza, Gramp, and something else I'd like you to try to like — here he is, Gramp, the new Burt Johnson I've mentioned."

Gramp didn't say a word. He threw the door open wide and stepped back and let them come in. Pete winked at Burt as they bustled about the kitchen making hot coffee and warming up the pizza and setting out plates and cups and saucers. Gramp waited in the living room until everything was ready and then with great dignity he made his appearance in the dining alcove where Pete had set out the snack.

"Gramp, you tell us where to sit," she said.

"There for you," he pointed to the side seat for Burt. "My granddaughter sits across from me and I sit here at the head of the table."

Pete kicked Burt's foot under the table, but she did not dare look at him.

The pizza was eaten in total silence. Gramp

studied Burt candidly throughout the meal. When he had finished, Gramp wiped his mouth with his napkin, set it down on the table, and swiveled his captain's chair to face his guest.

"Pete is after telling me that you've traveled a bit, here and there, over the years. I would be interested to hear something about one of the places, if it so happens you have been there."

"What's that, sir?" Burt asked.

"An island called Nias, west of Sumatra."

"Yes, I've been there. I spent a few days there when I went around the world and went back again because it fascinated me."

"You liked it?"

"Yes. It's still quite primitive. Next to my own private Island, which every man has in his dreams, I think it is the most offbeat spot I've found."

Gramp leaned forward. "You were saying something about every man wanting his own Island. That is the truth, the God's honest truth it is, and you know something, son, if every woman on earth understood this simple fact about the man she lives with, she would have a much easier time handling him, and the world would be a much cozier place for all of us."

The laugh started small, between the two of them, but it grew, swelling in volume, and Pete, who had tiptoed into the kitchen with a load of dishes, leaned back against one of the cabinets and let out a long breath. "It's going to be all right," she said softly as she leaned down and stroked Pesky, Gramp's big fat calico cat. "Everything is going to come up roses from now on in."

CHAPTER NINE

After evening practices Burt would follow Pete's Porsche back to her house, park his car, get out, and walk with her to the rear door. Mom would usually be at the far end of the house in the den watching television and gabbing with whichever one of the boys happened to be there that night for supper.

So Pete and Burt would have a few moments alone to say good night. Sometimes he would give her a few parting words of advice about her game. Or he might ask a few casual questions about school or about her brothers and their families. Sometimes he would stand a moment or two holding her hand as he said good night, but never, not once, did he make a move to take her in his arms or kiss her. She began to think that the man who had taken her out to Watch Hill — the Marine Coast Guard spot — was a figment of her imagination. Or that the entire incident had happened to her in a dream.

When Burt left her she would go upstairs to her room and, like as not, wind up the toy cager that Scott had bought for her and watch it heave that tiny basketball in the perfect hook shot. "What's the matter with him?" she would ask the tiny figure. "Or would it be more proper to ask what's the matter with me? What did I do wrong the first time that he doesn't ask me out to Watch Hill again?"

That Saturday night there was another dance at Toth Hall. Once again Pete went with Connie, making sure that she had dropped a broad hint at Friday's session with Burt as to where she would be on Saturday night. Burt did not show. But Shawn did. This surprised her. He was late arriving, breezing in on the party around ten o'clock. Pete pretended not to see him, remembering the last time they had been together. Shawn did not attempt to cut in as Burt had done but he was waiting for Pete as she came off the dance floor. He took her arm and steered her out of the "ballroom." He did it so adroitly that she did not have a chance to protest until they were on the glassed-in porch of the clubhouse, a deserted spot lighted only by the distant spotlight that played upon it from outdoors. The strains of the gypsy orchestra were muted but not so much that Shawn could not take Pete in his arms and whirl her around the empty porch a few times. She pulled free of him.

"Shawn, you're impossible."

"What makes you say that?"

"Well, you are. How did you know I was here? Don't tell me. Let me guess. You bird-dogged me through an infallible communication system. You charmed Gramp into telling you."

"Negative. Mom's the guilty party this time."

"I thought we weren't going to see each other anymore."

"All right. I'll close my eyes and you close yours, like this." And he took her in his arms again and they waltzed around the room. "This way we're together but not seeing each other."

"Stop it, you nut." She eased away. "I've got to

get back to the dance floor or Connie will wonder what's happened to me. What are you going to do?"

"Go back with you, behave myself, and dance with you if you'll let me."

"You could have said all that inside."

"It wouldn't have been as romantic, or half as much fun."

"Come on, let's get out of here."

"Wait a minute. We came out here so I could say something I couldn't say in public."

"Go ahead then."

"I'm sorry about that day out there in the country. I am sorry, honestly. I was upset, I guess, the way you talked. I've missed you, Pete. Have you missed me?"

"Not especially. I've been too busy learning how to play basketball. By the way, how's your bucket shot going?"

"I'm trying it Monday. At Rockwood. Return game."

Pete whistled. "That'll be a test. The acid one."

"How about coming over to the game? We can do something afterward, a foursome, Connie and Bill if you like."

"No can do. We play two games ourselves next week. One is a night game. You know what that means in girls' basketball. Big league, brother, big league." She moved toward the door. "Come on, Shawn. This place gives me the creeps. It's too dark and deserted. Come on, let's go."

He came over and took her hands and pulled her to him. "In a minute." He put his arms around her and held her close, kissing her warmly.

She pushed him away. "That's very nice,

Shawn, but it's not the time and place. No kidding, I think we should go back." Reluctantly he followed her. But she could not lose him so easily. He danced with her straight through the rest of the evening. And they won the Lucky Number dance.

"It's the first time in my life I've won anything but a basketball game!" she exclaimed as she stared at the prize, a tortoiseshell compact. "This is a gas," she told Shawn. "I need it like a hole in the head. I never use powder. I'd rather have the cuff links they gave you. I could use them on my new plaid shirt!"

It was, on the whole, a fun evening, despite the fact that she was still miffed with Shawn about a number of things. The four of them went out to the Green Comet Diner and had hamburgers and pie à la mode. Then Bill, who was doing the driving, since Shawn had left his car at Pete's house, drove them down to the shore for a look at the water and to do a bit of romancing. It was late when Bill dropped them off at the Phillips house.

"You better not try to come in, Shawn," Pete told him. "I don't want to wake Mom up."

"Just for a minute or two. Please. Honestly, I won't stay long."

"Like I said, you're impossible and a charmer, which makes you a double threat. All right, but just for a minute."

In the back entry, he put his arms around her again and snuggled close. "Pete, I did miss you. That wasn't eyewash. I'm crazy about you, Pete. Let's go steady."

"We fought about that once. Let's not start the rhubarb again."

"It's Burt Johnson, isn't it?"

"Now what do you mean by that?"

"I know. Word gets around. We're all in the basketball fraternity, aren't we? I've heard."

"What have you heard?"

"That you're with him every night."

"Of all the — ! With him every night! I'm practicing, *practicing* basketball at Bamberger Hall under the coaching supervision of Mr. Burt Johnson who happens to be also the coach of the Central High team on which I play the position of forward. That's how come I'm with Mr. Johnson several evenings a week."

"I understand he was quite a guy when he was a kid. A real hell raiser."

"So what? People change. Sure, he was a hell raiser and everyone knew it, but now he's an interesting and fascinating man, who has been a lot of places, seen and done a lot of things, tasted life, and is richer for it. He has warmth, compassion, understanding, experience . . ." She stopped.

Shawn stared at her for a long moment.

"You're in love with the guy, Pete."

"I am not in love with anyone."

"Yes you are. You're in love with Burt Johnson." He looked at her and shook his head. "I've suspected it for quite a while. Girls never know about themselves, how they really feel. Guys do. Guys make up their minds. Gals don't. They're afraid. Anyway, it's true. You love him. And what makes it so ironic is that I love you. I honestly do, Pete. Love in profile. It's an old story. The people we love often love someone else."

He went over to the glass door and with his finger drew three hearts. "Shawn loves Pete and

Pete loves Burt." He turned. "Never mind. I don't hurt easily. Disappointed, yes, but not hurt." He reached in the pocket of his jacket and pulled out an envelope. "Here. This is for you." She started to open it. "No, not now. Later, after I've gone." He pulled her to him once again and kissed her. With that he turned, banged his way down the steps, and slipped and skidded along the icy ground toward his car.

In her room, Pete closed the door and leaned back against it for a moment, staring down at the envelope in her hand. Something bulky inside. She opened it and saw that Shawn had slipped his cuff links, the ones he had won at the dance, into the envelope along with some snapshots. She took the pictures out and walked over to her desk. There were three of her, squinting up into the sun, and one of Shawn. A good likeness, all the charisma of the boy showing forth in the thrust of the head, the big smile, the merry eyes.

He's a winner, she thought. She said it to the four walls. "Shawn's a winner." She thought about their conversation, the last one, in the back entryway.

She could see him in her mind's eye, drawing those three silly hearts with his finger.

Shawn loves Pete and Pete loves Burt.

Love in profile. It's an old story. The people we love often love someone else.

She thought, I wonder who the gal is in Burt's life. Surely there is one. There has to be one. She felt a strange new sensation. Fear, envy, possessiveness, insecurity. Who is she? Pete kept asking herself. I want to know.

Or maybe there isn't anyone. Maybe.

She went over to the bureau to set the cuff links down on her dresser tray. Then she saw the note propped up, so she would not miss it when she took off her class ring and the ID bracelet her brothers had chipped in to give her when she entered high school. Every night she put her ring and bracelet on the tray, so her mother had known she would be sure to see the note.

"Pete. Mr. Johnson called. He asked for you to meet him at Bamberger Hall tomorrow around three. Don't bother to call him *unless* you cannot make it. If he doesn't hear from you by noon tomorrow, he'll expect you to be there. He said it was important. Good night and sweet dreams, dear. Mom. P.S. He does sound real nice, Pete. I thought you would want to know."

Pete held the note up and reread it. Tomorrow at three. And important.

She picked up the mechanical cager and wound it up and set it going. As she watched the doll heave a shot, Pete said, "Okay, Drusilla, you tell me. Am I in love with the guy, like everyone says I am?"

CHAPTER TEN

On Sunday the Phillipses had family troubles which detained Pete, so she was late getting to Bamberger Hall. It seemed that everything which had been pending by way of a family brouhaha came to a head that next day.

Paul's wife came over, full of grief over the divorce and wanting to weep on Mom's shoulder. In the middle of *that,* Lee burst in asking if anyone had seen his son Rex. "The kid's disappeared," Lee kept shouting. "His best friend, Wally Stivers is gone too. They've taken one of the Stiverses' cars. It's a mess."

Pete was not surprised. Rex had been getting into so many fracases at school the last couple of weeks, that she shuddered every time his name came over the PA.

In the middle of it all, Bud came barging in. Bud had not been home in months. Lee, upset over his kid, had wheeled on Bud. "Fine time to come home, when we're all having troubles. What do you want?"

"That's a great way to be greeted when you come home for the first time in ages." He mimicked Lee: " 'What do you want?' "

"I bet you want money."

"What if I do? Doesn't everyone?"

"Some of us get it by the sweat of our brow."

"Who's brow — yours or brother Tim's?"

"Don't get fresh."

"You started it."

The upshot was that Tim had to be called, and he brought over Mary and a couple of their offspring, and everyone stayed for Sunday dinner. Gramp was there, trying to restore some semblance of peace and spouting philosophy, and Tim was handing out free advice that no one listened to and was yelling at the top of his lungs that No, absolutely No, there was no more money going to be shelled out for Bud's scholastic ventures, debts, and subsequent dropouts. And all the women, including Mom, were crying copiously. And Tim's kids, of course, were screaming and running around all over the house.

It was awful.

Pete had to stay and help with the cleaning up, and calm Gramp down, and soothe Bud, and gently wallop Tim's kids a couple of times on their bottoms to make them shut up and stop breaking things.

So it was three thirty before she pulled open the side door of Bamberger Hall and started for the gym. She stopped stock-still in her tracks. When she had played basketball as long as she had, you had a quick reflex response to the noises in a gym. For instance, Pete could often tell without seeing the game, which team had the fastest drive. She could tell the quality of the baskets being made by the thump and whack on the boards. Sounds told plenty. The sounds issuing from the Bamberger Hall gym told her that Burt was not alone. Someone was in there tossing that ball with him. The someone was a girl. No matter how much like a man a girl moved and handled the ball, the *sound* of her

101

actions gave her away. And the girl was good. She was a seasoned basketball player who had a good dribble, a sure eye for the backboard, and speed. Lots of speed. Pete knew all this before she took another step.

Who in heaven's name has he got in there? Pete asked herself.

She walked slowly toward the door of the gym. The two of them were so busy at the basket that they did not see her standing framed in the doorway. So she had time to take a good long look. She knew the girl. Her name was Kaye Brown. She had transferred just three weeks ago from one of the roughest sections of a city in a nearby state.

Pete had noticed the girl when she was assigned to a couple of Pete's classes. You could not help noticing her. She was unusual. Everything about her was different from the girls Pete was used to palling around with. Her appearance was disturbing even to Pete, who was casual and, as Burt had put it, "a bit sloppy" herself. Kaye Brown looked as if she needed a grooming. Her fingernails were ragged. So were her clothes and her hair. The strange part of it was that she had an exceptionally pretty face if you looked behind the untidiness and the mask of hardness. The eyes were angry. She never smiled. There was a pallor to her skin as if she needed sunshine, lots of it.

Add to his the fact that she was a loner, not just a girl without friends, but a real honest to goodness loner who did not talk when you spoke to her, shunned the places kids congregated, ate her lunch by herself in a deserted corner, and would not meet anyone's glance.

She'll drop out soon, Pete had thought, watching her in the corridors and classrooms. She won't last more than a month in gregarious Central High.

Once or twice Pete had seen Kaye Brown standing in the doorway of the gym at school, looking in on the team as they practiced. And last week when they had played Wheeler High in the afternoon Kaye had come in to sit through most of the game. She sat off by herself, way up at the top of the grandstand and showed no enthusiasm whatsoever throughout the quarters, though Central High had swamped Wheeler with a nifty score of 60-27, and there had been some mighty fancy footwork and shooting on the part of the Central High girls. The boys who had come out for the game had been up on their feet a lot of the time, encouraging the girls, with a special notice to Pete, shouting at her, "Attagirl, Pete. Do your thing. You're in the groove again!"

It had never occurred to Pete that Kaye Brown was a basketball player. Yet there she was out on the floor of Bamberger Hall gym, slamming her throws into the bucket with a skill and ease that made Pete hold her breath and feel her insides going green with envy.

The stringy-haired, hostile-eyed kid was not only good. She was G-R-E-A-T.

Burt turned and saw Pete. She ran toward him, yanking off her coat and tossing it on the table. "Sorry I'm late. A family donnybrook," she called.

"That's all right. We've filled in the time." So now it's "we," she thought. And where did he find out about her, and how did he know she could play like that, and what does he intend to do about it?

He bounced the ball to Pete, who caught it easily. "Do you know Kaye?" he asked. "Kaye Brown?"

"Yes, we have classes together. Hi." Pete raised her hand in a slight wave to which Kaye made no response whatsoever. Dead pan, she stared a second or two at Pete, then bounced the ball, looking down at the floor.

"Kaye is joining the Central High team," Burt explained. Pete thought, How come I'm one of the captains and didn't get informed about it? He went on. "She played guard on her team where she came from. We need a guard."

"We've got three regulars, that's the customary number, which gives us the needed spare," Pete said. "Who's being shoved out to make room?"

"No one's being shoved out."

"Someone's got to be. Jinnie? You said she wasn't aggressive enough."

Burt looked uneasy, the way a man will when you try to pin him down. "No one's being shoved out, I said. We'll just gloat over having four good guards without going to the substitute bench. We're wasting time. Let's get moving."

That was an afternoon! At long last Burt deigned to work on basket-shooting. They tried every shot in the book. "First, we'll do the short shot," he said, "made from about six or eight feet from the basket without elaborate body action. Most short shots are best made from the left side, using the left hand," Burt told Pete. Kaye seemed to know this already.

Next they tackled the one-handed set shot, most popular of shots.

And then the running one-handed shot.

"You have to put reverse English on the ball for this one," Burt told Pete. "You should wait till you get to the peak of the jump before you flip the ball. It's all in the wrist action." Again Burt didn't seem to address himself to Kaye, since she was already performing the shot with ease.

They zipped through the two-handed chest shot and the two-handed set shot, but spent a lot of time with the jumper and the hook shot. Kaye Brown had a jumper that never missed and her hook shot was swift and deadly, aimed straight at the cage and whizzing right through, clean, neat, infallible.

They quit around five thirty, having taken a few breaks in between. Pete shrugged into her coat, wondering. She had not brought the Porsche over because with Bud home, for the time being, at least, she would have to share it. He had already appropriated it for this afternoon. She was sure Kaye Brown didn't have a car. No one in Bamberger Village was what you would call affluent, although most did fairly well in services and businesses shunned by the elite of Bradford. But Kaye Brown looked poor, really poor.

To which one of them was Burt going to offer a lift?

"Got your car, Pete?" he asked.

"Nope. Bud's home. Lend-leased to big brother."

"Come on, then. We'll all go together. I'll take you both home."

Which one first? thought Pete. She soon found out. Burt turned his car toward The Dockside. Even in Bamberger Village, The Dockside meant "poor." Once there had been a dock but now there was only a row of shanties in need of paint and with leaking roofs. Burt pulled up in front of one of them and Kaye jumped out. She looked at him and said, "Thanks." It was the first word she had spoken all afternoon.

"I'm going to get myself some bacon and eggs," Burt said as he drove on out of the Village. "Want to come along?"

"Yes, it will be good to steer clear of the Phillips homestead. All hell broke loose early this morning."

"What happened?"

She told him.

He took her to the little restaurant where they had eaten that first time, and she waited until he had finished his bacon and eggs before she asked the question uppermost in her mind.

"How did you discover Kaye? She's tremendous. Out of sight!"

"I saw her noseying in on the practices with a hungry look. And again at the games."

"So did I, but I didn't connect."

"She had the look of a basketball player. Tall, lean, good arms and legs. The way she watched the game and the practices told me something. I knew she'd never approach us, ask to join the team. I knew she was a terrified, lonely, lost soul."

"How did you know?"

"It takes one to know one."

"You were never a loner, not like Kaye Brown. You were a hell raiser."

"Same thing. We both had the same battle raging inside us. Alienation, hostility, bitterness. I handled my inside struggle by domination and aggression. She handles hers differently."

"She sure does."

"Don't sell that girl short. She's got deep feelings and has important things to say to her world."

"When is she going to start saying them?"

"Maybe after we draw her out."

"How did she get to be so great? Whew! What a shooter! If the guards — the defense men on her team where she came from — are that good, what about the forwards — they must break all records?"

"Her father was Hiram Brown."

"*That* Brown? The NBA All-Star defense man?"

"Yes. He taught her everything he knew until about a year ago."

"Till a year ago? Where is he? What happened?"

"I'm not sure. She won't talk about it. From other sources I found out that one day he just walked out on them. Her mother died of malnutrition and a broken heart. Welfare people rescued Kaye, brought her here to stay with her aunt. It's not much, but it's better than nothing."

"You make me feel — what do you call it — an empathy for her. Sort of as if I were in her shoes and know how it must feel and why she won't talk or look you in the eye."

"That's what I was hoping for. Now, let's change the subject. I'm ready to talk about my theory."

"You are!"

"Yes. You did well in the game against Wheeler High. No arm problem, right?"

"Except for a couple of times, but nothing to get upset over."

"You were relaxed. No problems. No one attempted to psych you. Home game. No heckling. Support from the stands, your own friends, chums, schoolmates, fans. You were shooting like there was no tomorrow. So it's an emotional problem, I was right the first time."

"That doesn't carry us any farther along to a solution."

"Not if we leave it there. But we won't. Pete, you're not going to like this, but I've got to say it. Your trouble is the way you think about yourself."

"The way I think about *myself*?"

"Yes. I know because that was my trouble too, only in reverse. I was the big I. The big Ego. Boss man. Everyone had to kowtow to me, the Big Man. With you, it's the other way around. You don't like yourself, Pete. That's wrong. You've got to begin by liking yourself or you can't make others like you."

"I thought I did about as well as anyone in that direction."

"No, you don't. It sticks out all over. That night at the big Southport game you took in every speck of garbage they wanted to toss at you, verbally, from the stands. You believed the stuff. I watched. I observed carefully. And when you're working with the team, you take the blame. Whatever goes wrong, it's you. You can be conned, Pete. Anyone can tell you you're no damn good no matter how great you are, and you'll believe it. That's all wrong. You've got to believe in yourself. Not just the self you've grown up with, but a bigger, inner self. A real person is lodged somewhere inside all of us who is capable of being noble and of doing important things."

"Where'd you get all this?"

He smiled. "Several places. You can't bum around the world a few times without discovering that the secret of making it is to raise your sights about yourself. Not egotistically, but with a kind of willingness to admit that we are all capable of being finer people than we think we are."

"Shawn Patrick talks a little like that."

"Yes, Shawn has found out."

"You're talking to me real deep, Burt Johnson. Someone must have talked to you like that too."

"You're right. It was a man I met in the South Pacific. A beachcomber, down on his luck. I bought him a meal and he talked to me. He said, 'Boy, don't make the same mistake I did. A long time ago someone told me to get a better feeling about myself, told me about an inner something that needs to be cultivated. I didn't listen. You, boy, I'm paying for my supper by telling you this and you listen, boy, you listen.' "

"And you did."

"I've tried to."

"Well, you have. You honestly have. You've made yourself over."

"I suppose you could put it that way."

"And it's like a chain reaction. Now you're telling me to change my attitude. Toward myself. To start to be different."

"It's a lot better than the way you wanted to

be different the other night. Copying someone else. All you have to be is yourself, Pete. Your real self."

They left the restaurant around seven thirty. "It's still early," he said. "Want to take a ride?"

"Sure, but not too late. Mom will be upset after all that mess and she'll need me."

He drove her out again to Watch Hill. No moon that night and they had to use a flashlight to make their way up the incline to the ridge. Burt stood looking down at the sea, holding her in his arms. It felt good. It felt wonderful. It felt right. When they went back to the car, they sat a long time in silence, holding each other's hands. And then without warning, he pulled her to him and kissed her. It was perfect. It was as if no one had ever kissed her before.

"Why did you wait so long?" she asked him. "I thought maybe you didn't like me."

"I wanted to wait until it would have some meaning, Pete. I didn't want it to be just another kiss."

It was around ten when he headed into the driveway of the Phillips house and got out to come around and open the door for her. The house was almost dark. Everyone had gone home. All the extra cars were gone, and so was her Porsche.

"I see Bud still has your car," Burt said.

"Sure. Bud's a scrounger. Gramp says every family has one. Bud's all right. He just hasn't found himself. Like you told me today, we've all got to work hard at searching for and finding the real us. Right?"

"Right." They walked to the back door and

Burt stepped inside. He took hold of her hands and pressed his lips against her palms. "You're a beautiful person, Pete. I don't mean the outside stuff, the glamour and all that. I mean really beautiful. The real McCoy. It goes deeper than surface things like a pretty face. It's something inside that makes other people feel important too."

"Thanks," she said. She laughed. "That's the second time today a girl has said thanks to you. It was the only word Kaye Brown spoke all afternoon."

"Pete, do me a favor, will you?"

"If I can."

"Help Kaye."

CHAPTER ELEVEN

Pete did not have much time to think about Kaye Brown and her problems on Monday. She had problems enough of her own. They began early in the day. During homeroom period Miss Vaughan called Pete to her desk and handed her a slip of paper. Pete read it. It was an appointment for her to have a conference with her guidance counselor, Miss Lucia, during Pete's fifth-period study.

She looked at Miss Vaughan. "What's this all about?" Miss Vaughan gave Pete her most sweetly sarcastic smile.

"When a prominent athlete is called into conference with the guidance counselor, Pete, what is it usually about?"

Pete didn't answer. She went back to her seat. It would be about grades, of course.

Pete fretted through Mrs. Maynard's history class and Mr. Webb's math class, glad only that she was not due to give a report in the former and that she was not called on to recite in the latter.

Her anxiety was monumental. This was the first time that her scholastic record was being challenged — if that really was the reason for the conference. And she was pretty sure that it was. Miss Vaughan's insinuation was correct. When a student active in sports was called in by the guidance office, it could be for one reason only — grades.

Pete tried to sum up her status so that she would not be completely unnerved when she was confronted by Miss Lucia's statistics. To begin with, she had been, until the last few months, an above-average student. She had a quick mind. She learned fast, and if it was true that fast learners did not always retain, what did it matter as long as she had the stuff when she needed it? But then something had happened. She had to admit that. The year had begun well enough and what she usually did was to build up a backlog of fine scholastic performances before the basketball season began — making sure that she did extra assignments, made a number of special reports, and boned up for tests so that her marks would be high. Then she could coast along when the heat was on and the ball was being banged against the boards and through the hoop.

This year it had just not worked out that way. She had continually run into a series of minor but disturbing episodes like that awful day when she had goofed on the Renaissance art report, had forgotten to bring the correct assignment to math, had really loused it up with Miss Vaughan by putting Connie's and her own ridicule of the sexy teacher on tape and gotten herself involved before an entire study hall in someone else's romantic episode! The last few months had been a repeat performance, although not quite so concentrated, of this same kind of oddball behavior.

Miss Lucia would know about it. She would have the records in a neat folder on her desk. And Pete had better have some good explanation — excuses, as such, would not help her much. Teachers were wise to the cop-out, the tendency to rationalize. "Don't make excuses" was one of their clichés, and the ability to cut right through the most artful excuses was one of the tricks of the pedagogue's trade. Pete knew.

Explanations were something else again. If they were valid, a compassionate teacher might listen and make allowances. It was best, therefore, to consider the background and disposition of the teacher Pete was going to be dealing with.

Miss Lucia was "one of their own." She had been born into, grown up in, and still lived with her mother and father and two sisters in Bamberger Village. She had graduated from Central High. For a while she had dated Pete's brother Bud. She was young. This was her second year at High. If Pete made a clean breast of her problems, spoke of the family embroilments, Paul's marriage, Lee's kids, Bud's insecurity and restlessness, Randy's business problems, Miss Lucia might listen and understand. Pete wouldn't have to mention how recently she had lost her father. Miss Lucia had attended the funeral.

By third period, English with Mrs. Ells, Pete had got herself fairly well calmed down and was able to pay some attention to the discussion of the modern American novel.

Mrs. Ells had just begun to phrase a question about the significance of Hemingway's title *For Whom the Bell Tolls* when the PA system rasped into her sentence.

"Pete Phillips, report to the office right away. Repeat. Pete Phillips, report to the office right away."

Everyone turned around. Pete got up. She

hesitated about taking her books. Connie, two seats behind, leaned forward and whispered, "Don't worry. I'll take care of everything for you, Pete."

When Pete entered the spacious outer office, Mr. Pryor's secretary nodded toward the inner sanctum and said, "Go on in, Pete. Mr. Pryor wants to see you."

Mr. Pryor got up and closed the door behind Pete. Standing in front of the glass door that opened out upon a small balcony was a man Pete knew well, and had known for a long time. He was Steve Harto. "Istvan" to his grandparents, who still lived in the old homestead in Bamberger Village. Steve was a lieutenant on the detective division of the Bradford police force. Because of his familiarity with the Village and its residents, Steve was more or less officially in charge of delinquencies and other problems connected with Central High. Pete had a sudden swift intuition as to why she had been called down to the principal's office.

"Hello, Pete," he said.

"Hi."

Mr. Pryor had a special small cough when approaching matters of some delicacy. "Pete, Lieutenant Harto wishes to ask you a few questions."

"What about?"

"I think it best that he introduce the subject himself. And because the nature of this talk is private, I think I shall absent myself from the proceedings." Mr. Pryor's formal manner told Pete that she was going to be put on the spot, but good.

Pete took a good long look at Steve "Istvan" Harto. He was a handsome man, pure Magyar, with the high cheekbones, the oblique shape to the eyes, the intense coloring. Ordinarily, he was a nice guy. She wasn't sure she was going to think so when she walked out of this office.

"Pete, as Mr. Pryor says, I have to ask you a few questions. About Rex, your nephew. He's been in enough trouble for ten boys. You know that."

"What do you want to know?"

"Anything that might help us straighten him out. We found him and the Stivers boy down in Maryland, heading south, in a car they took from the Stivers family."

"If he's back and the Stivers kid was involved and no one is kicking, then so what?"

"This much so what. Something must be going on in your brother Lee's home. Boys don't get so fouled up as Rex is unless there's a good reason, and often it can be traced right to the home. What's going on, Pete? Is there trouble between Lee and his wife? I know Paul's having that kind of problem."

Pete felt the fury rise. She wanted to lash out and slam Steve Harto across the mouth. She had to clench her hands into tight fists to keep her control. But somehow she managed to keep her voice to a husky, deep-throated pitch.

"You've got a nerve, asking me stuff like that. If you want to find out anything about my brothers, why don't you go straight to the source? Haven't you got the guts for it, Istvan?"

She saw his face go scarlet.

"I'm here on official business, Pete. I have

your principal's permission to question you. You better watch how you talk."

"I haven't said anything I wouldn't say in front of Mr. Pryor. And don't give me that 'official' bit. You're here because you need information and you're too chicken to face my brothers. You know that Tim would come into it and you'd be afraid of Tim, wouldn't you, Istvan?"

"Stop calling me Istvan."

"Very well, Lieutenant Harto. But don't forget, I've got Hungarian in me too. Grandma O'Hara was a Bogdany and that's about as Hungarian as you can get. I've also got some Italian, some Dutch, a nice parcel of Irish from the O'Haras, and, believe it or not, a speck of early American. Like you, Lieutenant, I've got a first name I'd rather not hear anyone else use. Petrina, from my Italian great-grandmother. And like you, Lieutenant Harto, I was born and raised in Bamberger Village. We stick together down there, Lieutenant, especially inside a family we stick together. Don't forget that, Lieutenant, the next time you decide to try to fish for information and pull a family apart by getting one of them to squeal on the other."

"All I wanted was to ask a few questions."

"You ask them. You ask the right person: my brother."

Pete did not go up to the cafeteria for lunch. She got her coat, and running up the stairs, pushed open the side door of the building and walked on up to the knoll that rose high above the rear of Central High School. The snow had melted and iced over. She slipped and slid on the path upward, but she had good boots and kept her footing. She turned around and looked down at the building. It looked what it was — an old dilapidated relic of a school building. She wondered what it had been like when it was new. One day long ago some teachers and students must have walked through those doors, proudly, into a brand-new building. Now, like everything in Bamberger Village, it was ancient history.

Now everything that touched Pete's life was old. The house she lived in, the furniture, or much of it anyway, the school. Yet she loved it all — the mellow maturity of it was something deep and precious inside her. It had meaning. It had a belonging.

Roots. Roots. That was the important thing. That was the thing that counted. That was what you never got away from no matter how far you traveled. Even at the top, if you got there, you dragged your roots with you.

When she came on down, Connie was waiting for her by the side door. "What are you doing? I saw you up there. What happened?"

"Never mind. I'll tell you later."

"Here, I brought you some sandwiches and cookies. And a carton of milk. You better eat."

"Thanks." She took the food and went on down to the girls' locker room. She put the stuff in her locker but did not touch it. Her stomach was sour. She would not have been able to keep the food down. The buzzer went off for the fourth period. She thought, I should be in economics. I don't even have a permission slip to stay out. I don't care. Suddenly it doesn't matter.

She wandered out into the lower hallway where the shop rooms were. She could hear Mr. Alexander's and Mr. Herbert's voices instructing the boys at the lathes or workbenches or millers. In the distance was the banging of tools as some kid poked around the "snakes" in the engine of the jalopy he was learning to work on. A boy came out, got a drink of water at the fountain, glanced at Pete, said, "Hi, you goofing off?" and went back to his job.

She felt tense, uneasy, unhinged. She dreaded the next ordeal, the confrontation with Miss Lucia. She tried not to think about it. She tried to think about what Burt Johnson had told her last night, the inner self, the real important self inside everyone.

Easier said than done, she thought.

She heard the buzzer for the fifth period and braced herself. I don't want to go up there to the guidance office, she told herself. I want to run away, anywhere. Anywhere that I could forget who and what I am. Only I can't. I'd take myself with me.

Miss Lucia's office was on the top floor, in a small room off the library. Pete knocked. Miss Lucia's throaty voice called "Come in." When Pete opened the door, she saw there were two of them, Miss Lucia and Miss Vaughan.

"Sit down, Pete." She sat, uncomfortably, on the edge of the straight-backed chair. She was thinking fast. I can't use any of the ammunition I prepared during those first two classes this morning. Not with Miss Vaughan here. It would fall flat on its face.

"Pete, this is by no means a reprimand conference." Miss Lucia's smile was enchanting. She was a pretty young woman with black hair cut gamin style and enormous blue-gray eyes from northern Italian ancestors. Small, slight, delicate of feature, she looked like one of the students beside the statuesque Miss Vaughan.

She went on. "We thought we should have a talk while there is still time to correct things."

"What things?" Pete asked.

Miss Lucia fidgeted and Miss Vaughan stepped in. "Your marks and attitudes."

"I know my marks have been better," Pete admitted, "but I don't understand what you mean by attitudes."

Miss Lucia got up, adjusted the shade, opened the window a crack, looked appealingly toward Miss Vaughan. Miss Vaughan shook her head. "Marie," she used Miss Lucia's first name, "this is your ball game. I think you're going to have to state the case first, and plainly."

Miss Lucia turned pale beneath her olive skin.

"Pete, I don't know quite how to put it. It's a change in the way you behave. Several teachers have reported trouble."

"Who? Who reported?"

Miss Lucia shrugged. "Well, there was that episode in the cafeteria."

"Oh, that. That was silly. It didn't mean anything. Mrs. Byrd gets upset over those study hall periods."

"And others."

"Miss Vaughan?" Pete looked at her homeroom teacher.

"I said others. Let's just leave it there. You're a senior now and I suppose this happens to prominent seniors. You've been a pretty big toad in the Central High puddle, Pete. Sometimes too much importance goes to our heads."

"I don't feel important. Most of the time, I feel very small and unimportant, like I don't know who I am or where I'm going."

Miss Lucia seemed to have no answer to that. She seemed also to be troubled about what she wanted to say next. She fussed with Pete's dossier, open in front of her.

"Pete, this is a highly personal matter and I approach it with some reluctance."

"What's a highly personal matter?"

Miss Lucia took the plunge. "Your going steady with a student teacher. It's a questionable thing to do, for the student teacher as well as for yourself. I'm not sure you are showing good judgment."

"Going steady! I'm not *going* with anyone, much less going *steady*. Burt Johnson is coaching me in basketball."

"Every evening?"

"Yes, every evening." She got up.

"Sit down, Pete."

"I don't think I want to sit down and listen to that kind of eyewash."

Miss Vaughan spoke up. "Miss Lucia told you to sit down."

"I'll sit down when I'm ready. I'm fed up, that's what I am. Burt Johnson is here to help Central High's basketball team win games. And I'm part of that team, and I've got shooting problems, and he's helping me iron them out. That's it and that's all."

"Is it, Pete?" Miss Vaughan leaned toward

her. "Are you sure you're telling the truth?"

She backed away. "What difference does it make? Sure, I'm telling the truth. It's no one else's business but mine, and even if I were interested in Burt Johnson as a man, it wouldn't be any worse than a teacher having a flock of boy students hanging around her desk morning, noon, and night, bringing her presents and driveling over her." That should fix Miss Vaughan!

She ran out of the office and out through the library. Kids studying or poking around the shelves looked over at her in surprise. She kept running, on through the hall, down the stairs, not knowing where she wanted to go, not knowing what to do.

She wound up in the only place she felt safe, the physical ed department. It was almost deserted. She had the locker room entirely to herself. No sound from the gym either. It must be a free period for the physical ed people, she thought.

While she slumped on a locker room bench thoughts raced madly through her mind. Wow, oh, wow, have I ever done it. Now, I have sealed my doom. Those awful things I said. Why? Why do I do things like that?

She sat there, shivering, wondering what to do. She couldn't go to her next class. It was Spanish with Miss Vaughan. Then she panicked at the thought that Miss Vaughan would probably send someone after her, to find her.

"I've got to get out of here," she said.

"Hello." She turned around, startled. It was Kaye Brown. "I saw you running in here. You looked upset. And frightened."

Pete was stunned. Yesterday at practice the girl had not spoken a single word. Now, she was not only talking, she sounded friendly.

"I've got troubles."

"Teacher troubles?"

"What else? That and some family problems too. I've got this nephew. He goes here — when he's not playing hooky or running away in a stolen car. They brought me into the act today, or tried to."

Kaye Brown stared at her for a long time, not speaking. "I know about troubles myself," she said. "It's one language I can speak and understand, without an interpreter either." Her smile was feeble, just a slight twitch at the corner of her mouth but it was a smile. "Know what I do when I get real low-down?" Pete shook her head. "I get out there on the basketball court and I slam them in, bang, biff, whack, thump, pound, pummel. Like the Queen of Hearts in *Alice in Wonderland*, I say to myself, 'Off with their heads!'" She smiled again, almost apologetically. "My father used to read me *Alice in Wonderland*. A million years ago, or so it seems." She came over to Pete and touched her arm, a light touch, like the brush of a butterfly's wing.

"Come on," she said, "the gym is empty. They don't have classes last period Monday. That's why I came down. I've got a free period too. Let's go in and make like we're the Queen of Hearts."

Pete followed the girl out. As they crossed to get themselves a bag of balls, she thought, What a switch. Burt asked me to help Kaye Brown find herself. Looks like she's trying to help me.

CHAPTER TWELVE

After Kaye's gesture of friendship, Pete planned a few overtures of her own. When she had classes with Kaye, Pete waited at the door for her, thinking they could walk through the halls together. But Kaye scooted off like a frightened animal. Because Kaye brought her lunch, she never went up to the cafeteria. So Pete got some sandwiches and followed Kaye up the path where, on not-too-cold days she ate her lunch outdoors by herself. That did not work either. Kaye saw Pete trudging up the incline toward the ridge and ran down another path, disappearing into the school building.

In the team basketball practices, Kaye showed a fine spirit of cooperation on the court. She was expert at passing, never hogged the ball, worked well with the other girls on strategy and playmaking. Yet it was perfectly obvious that she did not care to fraternize. Pete spoke to Kaye every chance she got, but Kaye's answers were monosyllabic and she would quickly back away. You would never believe she was the same girl who had befriended Pete on that afternoon in the locker room when Pete's world had nearly collapsed around her.

Nor did Kaye show up again for the special practice at Bamberger Hall with Burt Johnson. This surprised Pete. Burt was not only attractive, he had also proved that he had a special ability for coaching girls. So why hadn't Kaye taken advantage of the opportunity to receive more of Burt's help?

"What's happened to our protégée?" Pete asked Burt. "I thought Kaye would be a permanent member of our club after last Sunday."

"She doesn't like to come out for evening practice. Her aunt might worry. As a matter of fact, Kaye doesn't need basketball therapy, Pete. The girl is tops."

"You're telling me!"

Pete stopped fretting over Kaye Brown. It's a waste of time, she told herself. As Gramp puts it: about 99 percent of the time nobody can explain the way people act. You have to accept people the way they are. Let's just say Kaye felt sorry for you for one split second of eternity when you were sprawled out, an emotional basket case, in the locker room. Kaye understood and empathized because she had been there herself. But it was a one-shot deal. She's back in her shell. So forget it, loose her and let her go.

She did. She concentrated instead on minding her own business, which was getting the twist out of that temperamental right wrist of hers and absorbing as much coaching help as she could from those extra practices with Burt. He was giving her some psychological as well as technical help with her game. During these evenings when they were concentrating on shooting techniques, he would deliberately try to psych her out as she ran under the boards and would play devil's advocate to every move she made.

"I know what you're up to," she told him. "You're training me to hold my own against heckling and badgering."

Once, in a fit of anger, she hurled the ball

toward him. It grazed his right arm. He reached back and caught it before it bounced to the floor. He stood there, hefting the ball and eyeing her before he spoke.

"That's better than turning the hate on yourself," he said. "But it's not good enough."

"Is anything ever good enough to please you?" she asked.

"One thing would be."

"Name it."

"I'd like to see you learn to fight with your mind. That's the best weapon anyone has. That's the trouble with being raised in Bamberger Village. We grow up trying to fight with a lot of useless weapons."

"Like what?"

"Hostility, violence, anger, bitterness. Hating ourselves sometimes the way you often seem to do. We lock ourselves into our own prisons, Pete. Climb out, over that wall, use your mind to do it. You don't have to go to pieces when you're attacked from the stands the way you did at Elmhurst the other day. Be mad if you like, then use the furious energy constructively — to hurl baskets with brutal precision."

She listened to everything Burt told her and she remembered and she tried. She had never worked so hard at anything as she did at trying to please him, to remake her game and herself. She breathed, ate, slept, dreamed, practiced, thought nothing but basketball — Burt Johnson's brand of basketball. She practiced every spare second she had, out in the cold, under the baskets hinged to the garage and barn walls of the old Phillips house, down at the public courts where she would stop the Porsche and jump out and toss a few in when the weather permitted. Or in the gym at school, during noon hours or periods when the place wasn't being used. She carried a basketball up to her room at night and hefted it this way and that, in the techniques that Burt Johnson had shown her.

Her wrist was responding. She was sure of it. They played another game with Beecham, a return contest at Central High, and this time she went clear through the four quarters without once feeling that nasty little twinge when she handled the ball for a hook or some other spectacular shot. She made fifteen baskets in that game. She was in the groove again. She began to feel great when she walked out on the basketball court. The old feeling. The drive, the call to glory.

Things were looking up. Even the set-to with Miss Vaughan and Miss Lucia in the guidance office took on a new perspective. She was doing better in her classes. Mr. Webb gave her an eighty-five in a test and Mrs. Maynard complimented her openly before the class on a theme paper she had handed in.

Things were really coming up roses once again.

Then came the Rockwood game.

The whole school was looking forward to it. There were two home games during the girls basketball season that stirred real excitement at Central High — the games versus Southport and Rockwood. This year Rockwood was scheduled first.

The stairwell to the girls' locker rooms was covered with battle-cry slogans like RAM ROCKWOOD and WIN, TEAM, WIN! The names of the Central High stars were plastered on three-foot posters in the corridors and in the gym. CLOBBER THEM, PHILLIPS! confronted Pete almost everywhere she turned during those tense days before the contest with Rockwood.

It was to be a night game. Points made would count toward the "most valuable player" award. The small Central High gym had been sold out long ago. Not only the students themselves were eager to see Rockwood clobbered. The enthusiasm spilled over to parents, relatives, friends, even to natives of Bamberger Village who had never had a single child attend Central High. For twenty consecutive years Rockwood had met Pete's school on this big gala night when the entire ghetto — or as much of it as could legally squeeze into the old gym without breaking the fire regulations — turned out for the shellacking. Generally it had, over the years, been just that — an overwhelming victory for the girls. Only three times during those two decades had Central High lost on home ground to the powerful team from across the county.

The two teams were evenly matched. Rockwood was not a ghetto team. It was a school that specialized in athletics. You would think the school had never heard about the current pressures to phase out team sports. Rockwood reveled in competition. The team members were handpicked for physical and psychological fitness, as well as for skill at shooting, passing, playmaking, offensive, and defensive tactics. But

more than that, every girl who made the Rockwood team had to have that special something
that made for top performance under the boards.
It was a team of superstars.

Aside from that there were the people who
backed up this glittering handful of expert players. The two Rockwood coaches were imports
from the Midwest where girls basketball was
glamorous and big. Rockwood scouted the good
teams of the state, teams like Central High, to
brief themselves on the strengths and flaws of
their rivals. When they met Central High in the
old gym that Wednesday night, they would be
ready for just about anything.

Pete was excused early from school that day,
along with the other members of the team. Burt
Johnson and Miss Loudon met with them for a
few minutes before they were dismissed. There
was little conversation. Everything that needed
to be said had been drummed into them during
practice sessions. Miss Loudon told them to go
home and rest. Burt simply said that he would
see them that night.

Rest, for Pete, was out of the question. From
long experience she knew that it would be worse
than futile for her to go up to her room and
try to relax. She would keep running up and
down the stairs, out to Gramp's, and pace around
the yard, wearing out both her legs and her emotions.

She was tempted to grab a basketball and have
a few flings at the hoop on the garage. She knew
she must not. She was afraid. Afraid that she
might feel that twist in her wrist which had been
behaving so well during the last few weeks.

Let it alone, she told herself. Never kick a sleeping dog!

She got in the Porsche and drove around the Village. She had thought of going down to the public courts, not to shoot, just to sit there and brood, but she thought that Shawn might have the brilliant intuition that this was exactly what she would do, and he would follow her. She didn't want to see Shawn. She didn't want to see Burt or Mom or Gramp or any of her brothers or Connie or anyone who would pull on her emotionally. She had a one-second crazy notion to ride out to Watch Hill, but she dumped that overboard fast. She circled the Village again and again. It calmed her. The familiar dwellings, the kids playing, or riding bikes or shouting, the women gossiping, the racket from a couple of garages and machine shops, a crow cawing on a rooftop, the shabby storefronts.

She had another wild notion and drove on down to The Dockside. Mudflats, shanties, sea gulls. She drove on past the shack in which Kaye lived with her aunt. She wanted to stop and see the girl and say something to her. She didn't know what. She didn't even know why.

She stopped at a telephone booth and called home. Mom answered. "Mom, I'm not coming back for supper. I'll stop at the diner for a sandwich and milk. And go straight on to school."

"You won't eat properly, Pete. You'll worry me."

"I'll eat enough. Honestly. I don't want to have to answer the phone. If Connie or Shawn calls, just say I'm going right over to the school. Okay?"

"Yes, Pete, I'll do that. Pete, we'll be there, Gramp and I, and Scott's coming tonight, and Paul said he'd make it, and Tim."

"I know. I know."

"Pete, good luck!"

She started to say good-by and said, "Mom!"

"Yes."

"I'm all right. Don't worry."

CHAPTER THIRTEEN

As Pete ran out onto the floor at the head of her team, there was a roar from the crowd in the stands. She listened to the cheer for the team, followed by outbursts of personal encouragement throughout the stands.

"Go, Phillips, go!" ... "You show them, Pete!" ... "Rack up the goals, Pete." ... "That's our Phillips!"

There was no doubt that night as to whether the crowd was with her. Rockwood had brought its fans, but it was a small cheering section compared with the whole of Bamberger Village!

Pete faded into the queue at the basket for the warm-up, shoving Connie and Angie ahead of her. She did not want to be the first one to toss the ball at the hoop. Her knees felt rubbery and her palms were moist. She had experienced this stage fright so often before that she knew how to cope with it. If she kept her cool, it would pass. With no immediate problems and with the crowd rooting for her, the tension would be temporary. Yet she still felt it as she ran to catch the ball.

She held the ball lightly between her fingers, taking dead aim for the backboard. A safe one, she told herself. Make it an easy shot. She knew it was good as it left her hands. It banked, plopped neatly in the cage. The crowd roared. "Attagirl, Pete." "That's the stuff." "You show them, Pete!"

She tossed in a few more, then eased out of the shooting line on the pretense of some warm-up passes with Camilla Gomez, while she took stock of the Rockwood girls. She saw several familiar faces. She counted five veterans in the Rockwood warm-up line — girls she had played against last year and the year before. Like Pete, they were seniors this year. She reviewed her mental notes about them.

Number one on the roster was the tall skinny girl whose clumsy stance belied her potential. Her name was Heather Rose, a strangely romantic name for the plain-faced girl with too much nose, too little chin, and straight, stringy chestnut-colored hair pulled back in a thin ponytail held by an elastic band. Pete thought, Wow, what a case of deceptive appearances. That keg of dynamite looks like a dish of milk toast. There's the gal that does it all. Runs, rebounds, shoots, and blocks shots. Heather was known to her chums as "Grand Slam Rose" which was shortened to "Slammer." Slammer Rose. One of the co-captains of the Rockwood team. Slammer had no weaknesses to Pete's knowledge.

Next, Pete's gaze rested on "Wicket" Wickhome, Slammer's buddy. Same height but hefty, a fair-size Amazon, Wicket was a less versatile threat than Slammer but just as dangerous. She was what Pete called a ball hog. She had to shoot no matter what. Her hands itched for the ball. Some top-notch players would try to pass first and shoot if it was strategic. Not Wicket. Wicket would always shoot first and only pass if she thought someone would slug her if she didn't. Maybe not even then!

But ball-hogging gave her a fatal flaw. A girl

that ball-hungry could be exploited by the opposition to her own team's disadvantage. Pete racked up that weakness for future reference.

Then there was "Skid" Buckley, an adequate but not a phenomenal shooter like Slammer or Wicket. Skid had one enormous team asset. She was a dribbler, not just a good dribbler, but a great one. That coupled with an astonishing talent for passing made her an opponent to be respected. Practicing passes with Skid was a girl Pete had never liked. Pete could forgive the "court killers," the "hatchet men," the "grandstand egomaniacs." But one thing she could never stomach was deliberate temperament in a basketball player.

She flashed a long, hard stare at Pepper Wilcox and noticed that Pepper returned the stare before she tossed the ball to her pal Skid. Pepper spelled Turmoil and Temperament with capital T's. Pete had never played a game with Rockwood in which Pepper had not stirred up some kind of rhubarb, usually minor, occasionally crucial.

Last but not least there was the girl Pete had dubbed "Old Automatic" because of her record at the free-throw line. For this unfailing ability to make good on foul shots, Bobbi Walters had been nicknamed "The Robot" by her teammates. She was a short girl as basketball players went, around five-five, with thin spidery arms and legs and a face almost hidden by freckles, but the gleaming reddish-brown ferret eyes were worth a fortune to Rockwood.

"Ladies and Gentlemen: Tonight's starting lineup. For Rockwood: Forwards, Heather Rose and Janet Wickhome. Guards, Roberta Walters and Joan Buckley. Center, Marge Wilcox.

"For Central High." The cheers almost drowned out the voice on the PA system. "Forwards, Pete Phillips and Bretta Masi. Guards, Camilla Gomez and Tammy Kovacks. Center, Angela Alvieri."

Pete thought, So Burt is sticking to the regular starting lineup. She looked over at the substitute bench where Kaye Brown sat off by herself on the end, leaning slightly forward, looking down at the floor. Pete had had half a notion that Burt might push Kaye into the starting lineup, the girl was so good. He must be saving her as a surprise tactic.

"Ladies and Gentlemen: Our national anthem."

Pete stood at attention, slightly sideways, facing the flag and the speaker, and letting her peripheral vision flicker toward the front rows of the stands close by. She saw them all — Gramp, Mom, Tim, Scott, even Randy. Paul hadn't shown yet. He would. Paul was always late. And over there, close by the family, with Ross Plummer from Bradford High was Shawn, looking her way. She knew. She could *feel* his eyes on her. Someone else was looking at her too. He was standing close to the coach. Burt Johnson was staring at her, watching her. He's wondering if I'll make it tonight, she thought. He's wondering how I'll do.

The anthem was finished and she was in the huddle of coaches, captains, officials, not hearing a word, shaking a couple of hands without feeling the touch, feeling only that clammy something at the back of her neck, in her armpits, and the palms of her hands . . .

Then she was out on the court watching the ball as Angie jumped for the tip-off and the first quarter began.

Tammy passed to Camilla. Camilla dribbled, was blocked by a fast defensive spurt from Rockwood and had to pass off to Bretta. Pete clapped her hands for the ball near the keyhole. Bretta sent a high pass over the heads of the Rockwood defense. Wicket, Slammer, and Skid made a dash to intercept but Pete's reflexes were too quick for them. She aimed a one-handed set shot toward the rim. It rolled in. Goal and two points for Pete's team. The Central High spectators were on their feet screaming, "Nice work, Phillips!"

Wicket took the ball out-of-bounds for Rockwood. She tossed it to Slammer. Slammer fumbled and a groan went up from the Rockwood cheering section as Angie Alvieri was there to catch it. Angie looked for an opening. Pete's hands were high above her head, Angie let the ball sail over the heads of the Big D from Rockwood. Pete caught the ball, swiveled sharply, and aimed for the backboard. The ball banked and sank in. Central High 4, Rockwood 0. First minute of play.

Wicket took the ball out again. She feinted as if to pass it to Slammer but hurled it instead toward Skid Buckley. Skid dribbled down the court toward the Rockwood basket. Bretta was trailing her, Bretta's mouth going a mile a minute needling Skid. Skid dribbled sideways, behind, then in front, then sideways. She looked like a candidate for the Globetrotters. Suddenly Bretta darted forward and bounced the ball away, out of Skid's control. Skid stood for a split second, goggle-eyed with surprise. Bretta pivoted, looked for Camilla to be there for the pass. Camilla was hemmed in by Wicket and Pepper Wilcox. Bretta passed off to Angie who dribbled, hefted the ball, and sent it on a high hook pass to Pete. Pete was post-playing it, not because she wanted to but because the Rockwood Big D was all over the place, making it safer for Pete to stay near the keyhole. Pete caught the ball, turned, and started to aim a down-the-middle shot toward the rim, but Slammer was there, so Pete had to dribble around the keyhole to shake the tall stringbean from Rockwood.

No chance for anything but a short shot, Pete thought. No fancy body action on this one. She held her torso low, dribbled close to the floor, but kept her eyes up. Near the basket, she lifted her knee to get as much height as possible and stretched to carom the shot off the backboard. Slammer hacked at her arm just as she let the ball go. The whistle blew, but the shot was good. "Personal foul on Rose. Hacking," the PA rasped. The scoreboard clicked: Central High 6, Visitors 0.

The official motioned the teams to line up at Central High's free-throw lane and tossed the ball to Pete. Pete rubbed her hands on her shorts. She bounced the ball once, twice, three times. Placing one hand on top and one under the ball, sandwich-like, she let go for the target. It was a clean drop into the bucket.

The scoreboard clicked another point: Central High 7, Visitors 0. It was Rockwood's ball out-of-bounds and the Rockwood coach called time-out.

Burt came into the Central High huddle and talked in quiet whispers to Angie Alvieri; Pete couldn't hear, but it was probably some strategy for handling the defense. Angie nodded her head. Pete turned her attention to figuring out what was bothering the Rockwood Five tonight. No question about it, Pete did have the hot hand during those early minutes of the quarter, but there had to be something wrong with Rockwood that they let her get away with it.

They had a male coach, Al Gregory, from the Midwest, in that huddle with them. He looked angry and disgusted. So did Wicket. Something between Wicket and Slammer — usually close buddies. There was some kind of trouble brewing. Slammer had missed, or fumbled, or goofed in some way on that pass from Wicket. Pete had noticed that Slammer's reflexes were not the split-second reactions they usually were. Pete looked for bandages or some indication of any injury. If there was one, Slammer wasn't showing it off. Pete studied the way Al Gregory talked first to Wicket, then to Slammer. Wicket looked daggers, but Slammer kept her head down. Feuding, I bet, Pete figured. Between close friends at that. It happened once in a while. Over silly, petty things.

Al was trying to straighten it out.

He was instructing them, fast and positively. Pete watched his arm shoot out, saw the air, point first to one, then to another and another of the girls.

The horn called them back to the game.

The Central High cheerleaders came out on the floor and led a fast cheer for the team, finishing off with "Go, Phillips, go!"

Again Wicket took the ball for Rockwood out-of-bounds behind the end line. This time the pass to Slammer was good. Al Gregory had poured in some oil. They were team-playing, but good. Pete signaled to Angie to work for possession. Angie acknowledged. Pete got ready for a possible steal by the Central High center. *Then it happened!* Pete faded back toward the keyhole. Pepper Wilcox was right by her. When Pete ducked to the right, so did Pepper. Pete tried to dodge to the left, and Pepper was there blocking any possible passes.

They've put a chaser on me! Pete thought. The ball went to Skid Buckley, who dribbled down the court toward the Rockwood basket. Skid passed it to Slammer. Slammer to Wicket, back to Skid, who dribbled around the keyhole with the ball. There was a lot of action but every try for the Rockwood basket missed. Then Slammer got the ball, faded back for a long shot and made it nice and easy. A clean one into the bucket.

Central High 7, Rockwood 2.

There was a rally of cheers from the Rockwood rooters.

Camilla took the ball out-of-bounds for Central High. Angie signaled for a fast break that would bring the ball straight down the court to Pete at the keyhole. Pete was worried about Pepper Wilcox, but not too much. She had handled a chaser before. What Rockwood had done was simply to make an exception in their rule of all-court Big D tactics by putting a man-to-man defense on Central High's hot hand. There were ways to beat a chaser guard. Feinting, faking, using a lot of pivot and short shots, or backing off fast for a high overhead. Pete could think of half a dozen ruses that might work. She did not especially enjoy a confrontation with Pepper Wilcox, but if she kept her cool, she could outsmart the Rockwood firebrand.

Pete saw the ball coming. Tammy to Bretta back to Tammy to Angie, who jumped for a high hook pass to Pete. The second the ball left Angie's hands, Pete saw them coming — Slammer, Wicket and Skid. Heading straight for her.

Zone with a chaser! The phrase flashed through her mind. That's what they are doing to me!

It was the ultimate in the Big D. Putting four men on one forward. Pepper, their best defensive threat, had been assigned to press Pete under the boards. The other three would box her so effectively that she would not get a chance to shoot.

Pete accepted the challenge. She ducked back from the keyhole, with Pepper between her and the basket. Slammer, Wicket, and Skid had spread themselves out in strategic places, so if she moved for a court shot, they could tackle her from any spot. She had to do something and do it fast. She looked for one of her teammates to receive a pass. Tammy looked best. Pete started to throw toward Tammy, Slammer blocked. She tried for Angie, but Wicket blocked that pass.

They won't let me get rid of the ball unless I shoot! she thought. She pivoted and there was Pepper. Pete could not avoid contact. Unintentionally she pushed the ball into Pepper. Pete heard the whistle.

"Personal foul on Phillips. Charging," the PA blatted.

Pepper grinned as she hiked up her shorts and followed the crowd down to the free-throw lane. She toed up to the line, caught the toss, bounced, took aim, and let the ball sail. Plop.

Central High 7, Rockwood 3.

Again Camilla took the ball out-of-bounds and hurled it to Angie hoping for that fast drive to the basket. The drive was fast enough, but Rockwood repeated its aggressive blocking. Pete couldn't pass and she couldn't sink a shot. She let go a jump shot that bounced off the backboard, not touching the rim. Pepper got the rebound; the ball went down to the Rockwood basket. Slammer took it for a clean shot through the hoop.

Central High 7, Rockwood 5. The Central High cheering section clamored for action. "Make it this time. Go, Central, go!"

Once again the ball went to Central High. Tammy took it out and passed to Angie for a drive down the court. Pete wanted to shout to her teammates, "Get wise. It isn't working." She signaled to Bretta to try for a goal. Bretta dribbed too long. Slammer slapped at the ball for a quick possession. The ball went up the court again toward the Rockwood keyhole. Slammer tried for one of her long shots, but Angie blocked it and Slammer had to pass to Wicket. Wicket dribbled right, left, right, searching for a chance at a sure, easy shot. There wasn't any. She decided to use an overhead. With her back to the basket, she let the ball go right over her own head and the heads of the Central High guards, for a clean sweep through the hoop. That evened the score 7-7 and brought the Rockwood fans to their feet.

Pete thought, Why doesn't Burt call time-out? She would have called it herself except for one thing. She was too busy trying to handle her own end of a tough situation to know what to offer by way of advice to her teammates.

The quarter rammed on with Rockwood maintaining possession most of the time. If Central High got the ball, they either lost it or failed to sink a shot. When the horn ended the quarter Pete glanced at the scoreboard. Central High 7, Visitors 18.

Miss Loudon took the intermission huddle for Central High. Pete glanced over to where Burt was standing beside the scorer's table, his back to them. She wondered whether he had deliberately stayed out of the huddle because he was disgusted or whether he had withdrawn in deference to Miss Loudon's position in this big home game.

With Miss Loudon talking up things like "morale" and "team spirit" and "team cooperation," the two minutes were a total waste. Pete tried to figure things out for herself. She couldn't. She had been up against aggressive defensive tactics before, but never anything like this. A hatchet man sent in to rough her up was one thing. She came from Bamberger Village, she

142

knew how to deal with that. This was something else again. This was something she had heard about but never experienced. The total Big D. She had heard that it could win games. Tonight she was finding out, at first hand.

Angie, next to Pete, was puffing from the exertion of her ordeal in the first quarter. "It's awful, Pete, isn't it?" she whispered.

"Plenty tough," Pete agreed.

"What puzzles me is that they are letting you get the ball. You're the one they're out to stop, and the way to handle the big shooter on a team is to keep him from getting the ball."

Pete nodded. She didn't want to discuss it with Angie. She had wondered about that too, until she had figured it. It was a subtle effective strategy. The Rockwood team wasn't out to stop Central's ace scorer from *getting* the ball. They wanted her to get it and then have the frustration of missing. They were psyching her. A frightening fact dawned on Pete. They must have found out about her wrist. Somehow it had leaked out to Rockwood. They were letting her get the ball, so she could miss and go into an emotional tailspin over the frustration.

When Bretta got up from the huddle, she lost her balance and almost fell. Miss Loudon came right over. Burt Johnson joined her.

"It's my ankle. I turned it on that last play but I thought it would be all right."

Miss Loudon beckoned Connie off the bench. Burt Johnson looked as if he were going to say something. Pete had a pretty good idea what. He was staring over toward where Kaye was sitting by herself at the end of the substitute bench.

Pete thought, I wonder if he's figuring to send Kaye in as forward when she's a guard, playing strictly defense with us so far. Then she stopped thinking about Burt and Kaye as the second quarter started.

It began the way the first had ended, with Rockwood heavy on the scoring. They would let Pete get the ball all right and then block her when she tried to shoot. It was maddening. Once Connie got it and sank it for two points. And once Angie managed to connect for a goal with a running one-handed shot that made a spectacular throw. The Central High rooters rose en masse and shook the rafters with their cheers. Then back into the doldrums with Pete getting, trying, missing. When they were halfway through the quarter, the whistle blew for a substitution. Pete wondered who. She watched Kaye Brown run over to the official's table and report herself into the game. Maybe Kaye's coming in for Tammy or Camilla, Pete thought.

No such thing. It was Connie who went out.

Pete glanced at the scoreboard. 30-11 in favor of Rockwood. Pete didn't think sending in Kaye Brown could do much good with a lead like that.

It was Central High's ball. Kaye took her position in mid-court. Pete couldn't understand why. If she wants to break up the Big D block that's got me hog-tied, she should play nearer the keyhole.

The ball came down the court toward Pete as it had a couple of dozen times before. Kaye made no move to break up the Rockwood zone-with-a-chaser tactics. Pete pivoted as the ball hit her upstretched fingers, turned to try for a shot,

144

missed. She was bucking more than the Rockwood guards. She was bedeviled now by that crazy twist in her wrist. Pepper got the rebound, and the ball started down the court hell-bent for a Rockwood goal.

Pete, running toward the action, expected that Slammer would take the final pass and hurl in one of her long shots. Slammer did not get the chance. Kaye seemed to dart in out of nowhere. Every strong shooter had a favorite spot on the floor from which to make her baskets. Most of the time an ace forward knew how to get to this spot before the opposition could stop her. It was a matter of timing. Slammer had been having it pretty much her way.

Until now. Kaye's own timing was better than Slammer's. She arrived at Slammer's favorite spot and blocked. Slammer had one of two choices. She could hurry her shot and make a nervous miss at the basket, or she could move. She chose the latter. She moved. She missed. Kaye got the ball and started down the court. She was on target for a shot at the hoop just ahead of the moving zone defense from Rockwood. Maybe she'll hook it in, Pete thought.

Kaye didn't. She used a one-handed fall-away jump shot, releasing the ball straight out with fingertips and wrist. She shot like a hoopster who knows exactly where the basket is, more by feel than by aim. It was a perfect jumper. The Central rooters went ape.

The scoreboard flashed two points for Central High.

The rest of the second quarter went just about like that. Every time Rockwood got possession,

Kaye was there at the Rockwood basket ahead of everyone else to block the shot. Her timing was perfect. Then she would help get the ball to the Central High basket, so one of them could sink it.

The first half ended with the score of Central High 30, Rockwood 35.

Pete went down to the locker room for the intermission. She tried to conceal her feelings as the crowd of Central High girls went about the customary patch-up jobs required between halves. Her feelings were mixed — humiliation and hurt pride over the way Kaye had dominated the game, taking over and pulling the team out of a tight spot. It didn't do much good to tell herself that it was not her fault that Rockwood had devised a most powerful block against Central High's ace shooter.

More than that, she was concerned for the team.

Rockwood was nobody's fool. They had been taken off guard by Kaye's phenomenal skill during the last half of the second quarter. But during this intermission the heads would go together in the locker room next door. Rockwood was sure to come up with something.

Pete looked up from plastering a Band-Aid on her knee and saw Kaye standing in front of her.

"Hi, Pete."

"Hi, yourself. You did a tremendous job, Kaye."

"That's not what I want to talk about."

"What?" Pete asked.

"About the next half. It's not going to be as easy."

"That's what I was thinking."

"I'll need help," Kaye told her.

"What kind?"

"My father used to have a saying about how to win a game from tough opponents."

"Which was?"

"Get them *thinking*. Instead of letting them play their normal game make them start thinking. That will upset them and you'll win."

"How do we get them thinking?"

"Do to every player on the Rockwood team what we did to Slammer this past quarter."

"You mean what *you* did to Slammer."

"You're the team spark plug," Kaye went on. "Me, I'm no good at talking."

"You're doing just fine. Keep rapping."

"Every Rockwood player has her favorite spot on the floor for shooting, or has her strong point in playmaking."

"Like Skid's dribbling."

Kaye nodded. "You playmake for the rest of the team. Tell the girls how to handle themselves, what to do to upset the Rockwood Five."

"That won't win a game. With all due respect to your father."

"Not by itself, but I've got more ammunition."

"I can't wait to hear."

"Keep your eyes open when we go on up and you'll see." She started to move off toward the door.

"Kaye," Pete called her name. She turned. "I had no idea you could be such a chatterbox. You turned out to be a real Gabby Gertie."

The grin started small but it widened until it lit up Kaye's pale features. "Like my father used to say, I'll see you on court!"

Kaye's strategy worked. Rockwood came back

into the game looking worried. They now had two ace shooters to block. It wasn't the same ball game at all. By the end of the third quarter, the score was tied 43-43. Kaye's tactics had not only enabled Central High to rack up points but they had held the Rockwood Five down. Kaye's method was simply to funnel Wicket and Slammer, the big shooters, into the middle and keep them there with a resulting poor percentage of shooting for that duo, while Angie and Tammy got the rebounds and delivered them to Kaye and Pete at the Central High basket.

In the two-minute intermission before the last quarter, the Central High girls huddled in a circle and tried to catch their breath. Most of them were puffing hard. It had been a tough eight minutes of play. There was little talk. Pete was glad that neither Miss Loudon nor Burt Johnson harangued them with advice. They needed rest, not talk.

Pete had her own private concern. Her wrist was not only twisting. It ached. She had given it a wrench during the final play of the third quarter when she had pivoted for a short shot to the basket.

Kaye was dominating the game, no mistake about that, and she did her share of the shooting. Her jumper was fabulous. But Rockwood had closed in on her toward the end of the last quarter and they would continue to do so, more directly, when the pressure of the final minutes of the game was on full blast.

The horn called them back to the court.

Pete took her place near the keyhole, still post-playing it. She tensed in response to the excitement in the stands and to the noise in the gym. It was heady stuff, music to the ears, but hard on the nerves. She heard her name called from half a dozen spots in the stands. "Keep sinking them, Pete . . . Go, Phillips, go . . . Give us a victory, Phillips . . . Stick with it, Pete." The cheerleaders bounced out on the floor and bellowed through their megaphones "Let's have one for Phillips!"

Then the ball went into play for the final quarter. Rockwood got the ball and began their drive toward the basket. Angie slapped the ball from Skid's dribble and hurled it to Tammy who passed to Camilla. The ball came down to Pete and Kaye at the basket. Pepper had taken the pressure off Pete and turned it on Kaye. So Pete had to receive the pass for the shot at the rim. As the ball hit her fingers, she felt that nasty twinge in her wrist but she couldn't pass off. She had to shoot. She let it sail. It plopped in, neat and clean, not touching the rim.

Central High 45, Rockwood 43.

Then Rockwood got the ball and held it. Skid dribbled the length of the court and did not wait for Slammer or Wicket to catch up with her. She sank it herself.

Central High 45, Rockwood 45.

The stands were out of their skulls with tension. Pete felt bombarded by the horns and noise-makers, the screams of "Go, team, go!"

For the next few minutes of play, the game went like that. First Central High would score, then Rockwood. The score tick-tocked. It was a game on a seesaw.

As they went into the last three minutes of

play the scoreboard read: Central High 54, Visitors 54.

The fans were on their feet screaming their lungs out. Then it happened. Slammer and Tammy jumped for a pass at the same time and collided head on. Both girls went flying. For a second all you could see was a mass of arms and legs. Whistles blew for time-out. The officials and coaches came into the huddle. Tammy jumped up, but Slammer was still on her back.

Someone in the stands shouted, "She's out cold."

She wasn't. But Slammer had been hurt. It took two of them to help her off the floor and over to the Rockwood bench. A tall blond came in for Slammer. Pete didn't know her name. All she knew was that the girl was not Slammer Rose.

The two-minute horn blasted them into the final minutes of the game with the score still 54-54. One thing is sure, Pete thought, nobody's going to beat that clock tonight!

It was Rockwood's ball. Skid got it down near the basket for a pass to Wicket, but Wicket couldn't maneuver into position for an accurate shot. She should have passed but didn't. She tried and missed. Angie got the rebound. Angie had the ball and was steaming on down toward the Central High basket.

The fans were still on their feet, screaming for a goal.

Pete jumped for the pass from Angie, her fingers closing on the ball for a firm grip. She pivoted and looked. Pete listened. The Central High rooters were chanting:

"Do it like the Army does, shoot it, shoot it.

Do it like the Navy does, sink it, sink it."

They were telling her it was the last half minute of play. She looked for Kaye. She wanted to pass off. Partly because she did not trust her shot, but partly because she felt Kaye was *entitled*. This had been her ball game. She had come in and sparked the Central High team to a whole new scene.

But Pepper was there beside Kaye. And Skid too. And the stands began chanting off the last ten seconds of the game. "Ten, nine, eight, seven . . ."

Pete wanted to give the glory shot to the girl over there with the pale face, the hungry mouth, and hungrier eyes.

But she couldn't. There wasn't time. There was only time to win. *If she could.*

Pete saw Pepper and Skid breaking toward her as they realized she was not going to pass off to Kaye. She faked a pivot to the opposite direction from which she planned to shoot, did a fast switch, dribbled, came to a stop, and stepped out with her fingers controlling the ball. Her right wrist twinged. But all she could think about was the board and the hoop. As she started to turn she kept her eyes on the basket, releasing the ball as smoothly as she could.

It's a good one, her own thoughts shouted at her above the pandemonium in the stands. I know it's a good one!

CHAPTER FOURTEEN

After the Rockwood game, Pete by no means felt at ease with herself. The Rockwood game had been Kaye's game, as Pete had known that night when in the last three seconds of play she had sunk one of her spectacular shots.

But the credit for the win had come to Pete.

For days she accepted her congratulations in Bamberger Village. The *Bradford Inquirer* carried the story on the sports page with the headline: "Central High Shades Rockwood Behind Pete Phillips."

The story was just as inaccurate in that it gave full credit for the victory to Pete.

"The Central High Girls Basketball Team registered its most important win of the season so far, edging out the visitors, Rockwood High, by the score of 56-54. Pete Phillips of Central High sank a long hook shot with three seconds remaining, to give her team a victory over Rockwood in the legendary gymnasium of Central High that has seen action for almost half a century. It was the traditional game of the year for the girls from Bamberger Village, since most of their relatives, pals, and friends had turned out to see Pete Phillips lead her team to victory."

The other girls on the team were mentioned briefly, including Kaye. "A newcomer to the team, Kaye Brown, daughter of Hiram Brown, the former NBA champion, made a good showing with a unique jump shot."

That was all. Pete, rereading the article, said to herself, It's not enough. Kaye Brown had dominated that game. She had come into it when there wasn't a cockeyed chance of Central High being anything but swamped. She had worked a miracle. She had given the team everything she had: her fabulous jumper, her marvelous timing, her cool under pressure, her playmaking — psyching Slammer and holding the Rockwood star shooters funneled in the middle. In addition to the asset of her poker face.

Pete had learned a lot about Kaye Brown in that game that she had not known before. She was not a polite player, this girl from The Dockside. On court, her personality changed from mouse to lion. She played for keeps. She worked every minute of the game. When she couldn't jump the ball in, she shoehorned it into the bucket. She was incredible. She reminded Pete a little of a talented actress who had come onstage in a bad play and turned it into a smash hit.

But the glory had come to Pete — if not all, certainly the largest portion of it. Much beyond what Pete had earned in that game. All around her was talk about a Most Valuable Player award. Funny thing about fame or celebrity or whatever, when it hit, it hit hard and everyone wanted to jump on the bandwagon.

"I owe Kaye Brown," Pete told herself. "I'd better make the overtures once again and see if I can yank her out of her shell."

The midwinter vacation began the week following the Rockwood game. Burt told Pete that he would have to be away for most of the week, to go up to college and clean up on some term papers, work that had nothing to do with coaching Central High's team. "You don't need my personal help now, Pete. I think we've covered as much ground as we can. If Miss Loudon wants to call practices, that's up to her."

They were sitting in the car out at Watch Hill where they had driven to be together for an hour or so. Pete looked at Burt's profile as he stared straight ahead, deep in thought. In his rugged way, he was still the most handsome and exciting man she had ever known. She wanted to tell him that and a lot of other things. She wanted to say, "Burt, I'm going to miss you more than I miss even Hoyt or Scott. Not just because of all you've done for me but because of you, the way I feel about you."

She couldn't say any of it. Instead, she sat in silence, a silence Burt had to break himself.

"You'll be busy with friends all week, Pete. I hope you won't forget me while I'm gone."

"I would never do that." She had a hard time squeezing out the words.

"Besides working on my college stuff, I'm going to do some serious thinking while I'm up there. Personal thinking about things important to me."

She didn't answer, unwilling to probe. He went on. "Pete, you're serious as an owl. What's on your mind?"

"Kaye Brown. The raw deal she got in the game. The deal I dished out to her by not heaving her the ball for that final shot. I was worried that she wouldn't make it or something would happen to goof up the win. We needed those two points, and I chickened out on giving it to her. That's what I told myself. But I was rationalizing. Kaye could have made any shot from anywhere, anytime."

"That's fallacious reasoning, Pete."

"Translate."

"You're fouled up on your logic. Funny thing about you, Pete, you try to be rational so much of the time and then when you begin to figure anything out, you turn illogical, emotional."

"Well, it wasn't just that final glory shot that I swiped from her. It was other things. The newspaper story, all that razzle-dazzle about Pete Phillips — the great star I was in that game — when you know and I know that a lot of the time my performance stank. Even writing about the prominent Phillips family, dragging my brothers into the act, how great they were as stars, and giving me the reflected glory. It was awful. It wasn't fair to Kaye. I'd like to make things right."

"Then do it."

"How?"

"Go on down and see her. She's on vacation same as you and probably bored and lonely. Go ahead."

"She'll run away. I've been thinking of going down, but you know how she is, no one is welcome. No one."

"Try it and see. 'Nothing ventured —' you know the rest."

"I suppose I could."

"Sure, you could. Anyone can do anything if he wants to badly enough." He took her in his arms and kissed her before they left Watch Hill. "I'll try to get back for a date later in the week. Don't let the competition get too tough."

It was a day almost like spring when she got in the old Porsche and drove on down to The Dockside. There weren't many children out playing down in that section of the Village. The warmth, the vitality of the ghetto, the sounds and smells she loved, these she left behind as she turned down toward the waterfront. The smells here were not of Italian and Hungarian cooking, but of the musty dank odor of mud flats at low tide. There was the bleat of sea gulls instead of the warm cries of children at play. Down here were the lonely oldtimers, the forgotten people, self-imprisoned behind sagging shades and bolted doors. Kaye's aunt did housework up in Bradford by the day. Pete had pictured Kaye sitting alone in a darkened room watching television. So she was surprised as she turned down the street to see Kaye outdoors, bundled up in heavy slacks and a couple of sweaters and hurling a basketball into a decrepit looking hoop attached by new hinges to the side of the shanty.

Pete pulled up and sat in the car, thinking, I'll wait and give Kaye the chance to call the signals. She knows the Porsche. She'll know who it is. Maybe if I let her take the initiative, it will work.

Pete sat several moments. Kaye kept slamming the ball into the basket. Finally she turned and, bouncing it as she came over, approached the Porsche.

"Hi," she said.

"Hi, yourself. Want to take a ride?" Long pause. "It's such a great day, and I've got to run over to Southport to do an errand for my mother, and see my brother Paul. I was hoping you'd come along, Kaye."

"You've got a lot of other friends, what's the matter, are they all too busy?"

"I didn't ask them. I've been thinking about asking you, but didn't have the courage. You're not an easy girl to reach, Kaye."

She gave Pete a sharp look full of awareness.

"Come on, Kaye. It'll be a nice ride."

"I'll have to leave a note for my aunt — she gets home early some days — and get my coat from the house." She started bouncing the ball on the way to the house, then came back. "You honestly want me? I mean, it's not just that you're sorry for me or like that?"

"How could anyone feel sorry for a girl who can play the kind of basketball you played the other night, Kaye? You're far better at the game than I am, so where's the feeling sorry, No, I honestly would like your company."

The ride out to Southport was not a gabby one. Whatever conversation there was, Pete had to keep it going. She was careful to stay on the casual, lighthearted side, impersonal topics like school, the kids, the team, the game, and never to probe or ask questions. After a while, Kaye began to relax. When they reached Paul's auto agency, Kaye warmed up, showing an interest in the cars, and a knowledgability that surprised Pete.

Kaye explained. "My father was a car buff. He taught me a lot about mechanics."

"Errands finished and mission accomplished," Pete said as they pulled out of the main stem of Southport. "There's a diner up the road and the inner girl is yelping for a hamburger. Okay? Could you go for one? The treat's on me."

Kaye didn't answer but she made no objections

when Pete pulled into the diner parking area. Pete had to order for them. Hamburgers, milk. "What kind of pie do you like?" she asked Kaye. "I like apple à la mode."

"I like pudding, rice pudding if they have it."

"Rice pudding for my friend," she said to the waitress. Inwardly, Pete was exultant. This was progress, for Kaye to stipulate a preference. A little aggression, Pete thought, is the first sign of freedom!

While they were eating their dessert, Kaye looked over at Pete and said, "I guess you wondered why rice pudding instead of pie."

"No. Like the French say, *Chacun à son goût.*"

"I bet you thought I wouldn't know French. My father spoke it. He spoke Spanish too. He was in the Navy. My father knew a lot of things." She paused and looked at her pudding. "That's why I ordered this. We — my father and I — we used to go to diners and restaurants a lot, and he liked rice pudding, and that's how I got to like it too."

"I bet he took you to a lot of places, Kaye."

She nodded. "Hockey games. He was crazy about ice hockey, and my mother didn't like spectator sports. She wouldn't even go to see my father play basketball. He'd take me when he could and was playing anywhere near, and I'd have my special spot near the front, and he'd come over and talk to me, and the other players made a big fuss over me. Once he took me to an art gallery, and lots of times to the museums, and to plays — real plays onstage."

"He sounds like an interesting man. I know he was a great basketball star, but nobody ever knows what the man behind the hook shot is really like."

"That's the trouble. That's what's wrong with everything. I mean where famous people are concerned. My father used to call the grandstand crowd 'the Great Dark Beast.' He said he got that from some actors and actresses he knew. They called the audience that — the Great Dark Beast — and said it could make you or break you, that it could be cruel or bitter or dull or bored. And it had a terrible appetite for celebrities; it had to have its glamour gals and guys. There was something in human nature, my father said, that made it important for everyday kind of people to have heroes and celebrities, so that first they could build them up and then tear them down. He said, God help the victims, the famous ones who had a small brief day in the sun and then got tossed into oblivion." She paused, suddenly covered with that rather charming shyness she had shown before. "Look, the way I've rattled on, when you aren't even interested."

"Not interested! I'm fascinated, Kaye."

She took a long look at Pete. "Could I say something?"

"Sure, why not? Go ahead."

"Pete." It was the first time she had used Pete's name. "Pete, you're a nice person. I mean, honestly nice. Not gushy and putting on an act. But down underneath you're swell. I never thought I'd say that to anyone again. The way I've been feeling, all choked up and bitter inside. Hurting so hard that the bitterness is a taste in my mouth. I promised myself that never, never

159

again would anyone get even a little bit close to me. I guess it's because you are the way you are, blunt, direct, honest, putting everything on the line, I guess that's why, well — to put it your way, that's why I've let you reach me."

That ride to Southport was a beginning.

Every day that week Pete drove down to The Dockside to pick up Kaye. The weather continued to be bright and mild for that time of year. Pete always had some family errands to do and would invite Kaye to ride along with her. Pete began bringing Kaye back to the Phillips house. She stayed for supper. On Randy's night for having supper with Mom, Kaye was fine, talking about the restaurant business with real interest. "My father's best friend owned a chain of eating places," she explained.

But on Tim's night, Kaye maintained an almost absolute silence, speaking only if directly addressed and then keeping her answers to short terse sentences.

"You were different tonight," Pete told her afterward.

"It was because Tim reminded me of my father."

"Tim! How could he? Tim's so down-to-earth and not a bit glamorous. The way I remember reading about your father, he was a celebrity type — always smiling into cameras, a showman."

"Not really. That was what you called the mask. When we were alone he was like your brother Tim, hearty and wholesome, making you think everything was right with the world."

She grew quiet, then went on. "That's why I was so silent tonight. I remembered Dad the way he was before fame spoiled him."

"Can you stand to meet another man like that?"

"Who?"

"Gramp. He can't wait to meet you. I've been telling him about you."

"What's there to tell about me?"

"That you're a better basketball player than yours truly. Gramp doesn't believe it. Come on, everyone I bring home has to pass the acid test. You might as well get it over with."

They had supper the next night with Gramp. Gramp warmed to the presence of the quiet, lonely girl and turned on his best charm. He sparkled. He told stories that Pete had heard a dozen times but they were still good and many of them were funny. It was the first time Pete had heard Kaye laugh.

That night after Pete had driven Kaye back to The Dockside she stopped again at Gramp's to help clean up. While they were stacking the dishes, he said to Pete, "I like that girl, Pete."

"So do I."

"She has something you don't find much in girls anymore. In my day, it was a feminine specialty."

"What's that?"

"Sweetness. Underneath that facade of reserve and some bitterness, there is a genuine sweetness of character."

"I know."

"She'd be a real beauty too if someone would take an interest. Did you notice her features?

They are delicate and fine. And her eyes are something old-fashioned poets used to write about."

"I believe you are referring to 'great dark limpid pools.'"

He turned, looked for the twinkle in Pete's eye, she winked at him and they both had a big roaring laugh about it.

"Gramp, you're a sneaky old scalawag, and don't think I don't realize what you are getting at. You want me to help Kaye dress and fix herself up, right?"

"Last time I heard, you had a bunch of stuff that you'd grown out of and were too attached to to part with. That girl is just the size to fit into something you've grown too plump to wear."

"Grrr. I hate you, you insulting monster. Haven't you heard no woman wants to be told she's too fat for her clothes?"

"Plump is definitely not fat. It is pleasing to the eye of the male of the species, my fine well-set-up granddaughter."

"Enough outrageous flattery. As for your suggestion, it's impossible. Kaye is proud. She's just beginning to open up and become a member of the human race from which she had resigned when I met her. If I start offering her hand-me-downs, it would be the end of a beautiful friendship."

"Not if you do it right."

"How does one do it right?"

"Let's see, if I were my granddaughter, I would suddenly get the bright idea to have a party. Now, over there is that big house which used to have parties when your brothers were home, the rugs would be rolled up and the old floors are great for dancing and there's a brand-new stereo your brothers gave your mother for Christmas and a piano, which is tuned up just fine because Tim and Scott and your mother still play it. Then I would invite all the friends I've got like Connie and that oddball she runs around with, and Camilla Gomez and Tammy Kovacks and the others, and their young men."

"And Kaye Brown? You think she'd bust out of that iron fortress she's bound herself into for a party? You've got to be kidding, Gramp. She's just beginning to peek over the top of her prison bars. She'd be overwhelmed at a bash like the one you're planning."

"I don't agree at all, at all. She's hungry for people. Afraid, timid, reluctant to take that first plunge, sure and she is that. But give her the incentive, the first push, and she'll jump in. Try it and see. And the first thing she will say when you tell her about the party is, 'I haven't a thing to wear.' It is what every woman says, even if she has four rooms for clothes like some famous actress admitted on television the other night."

Pete went over and gave him a kiss.

"You're the world's smartest man where females are concerned."

"That I am not. It is simply that I was married to one."

CHAPTER FIFTEEN

When Pete spoke to her mother about it, she met with wholehearted enthusiasm.

"Why, Pete, that's a marvelous idea. I'm so glad Gramp thought of it. February is a bleak month. A party will liven things up."

"It's just for the basketball team and their boy friends, Mom. I guess we'll have to invite the whole varsity including the substitutes. It would be around fourteen couples. And some extra boys — maybe half a dozen — just in case. You think that's too many?"

"Of course not. Scott and Bud used to have twice that many here." Her mother's expression was wistful. "Those were the happy days. It seems so long ago." She brightened. "But the present — now is all that counts, and we'll make your party a happy time too." Her mother, practical as always, began immediately to talk about plans. "Randy will take care of the refreshments — he's done a lot of catering. And I'm sure he'll let me borrow Dusty for one evening." Dusty was Randy's wife. "And Mary will give us the whole day. You know how Mary is, she'd be hurt if we didn't ask her to help with everything."

"I can help too, Mom. It's vacation. And Connie will pitch in and so will Camilla and Tammy. And Shawn, if we need a strong male arm."

"Whoa, Pete. Slow up. Too many cooks spoil the broth." But her mother laughed heartily, and that was a great sound to Pete's anxious ears. It was decided that Saturday night would be the best.

"It's such short notice. But Saturday is a night everyone dates anyway. And I think most of the girls will accept."

Pete called Connie first.

"How'd you like to go to a real jamboree?"

"Where? Who's giving it?"

"Me, here at the Phillips estate."

"You're kidding. No, you're not. Lately, you've sprung so many surprises, one more shouldn't throw me. Who's coming?"

"The whole varsity. Subs and all. And their guys."

"That's no jamboree. That's a Mardi Gras. We haven't won any championships yet. So what's the occasion for the big bash?"

"Can you keep it confidential?"

"I can try."

"It's a sort of debutante party, an introduction to Bamberger Village society for Kaye Brown."

"Kaye Brown! Pete, I'm beginning to think you *are* whacked out of your wig. Kaye won't even talk to us, no less let us give a party for her."

"She's not going to know it's for her. That's the secret. Gramp had us to dinner the other night and he liked her, not just a little but a whole lot. She's lonely and frightened, Connie. While you've been busy helping Bill with his business this week, I've been gradually scooping Kaye out of her shell. It isn't easy but it does look promising. She's had meals with us several times. We've gone over to Southport, to Paul's, and she's a whizz about cars. Her father was a buff.

He's her hero. She had a real companionship there before the bust-up. I think he was probably a very nice guy before success phased out the man behind the public image. Anyway, the party was Gramp's idea. He suggested it as a way to help Kaye."

Connie was from Missouri. "She didn't impress me as wanting to be helped. Hands off seemed her motto, Pete."

"I know."

"Then why the sudden interest?"

"At first, I did it because I owed her. You know what I'm talking about — the Rockwood game. I got the whole credit, and a lot of it should have gone to Kaye. I mentioned that to Burt before he left and he said to square things away, to go to Kaye. It wasn't easy. But once I broke the ice, she warmed up. She's interesting. Her father took her around a lot, and beneath that crust of 'stay away, I hate you' is a different girl. Keen, interesting, and a nice person."

"If we're to bring our own men, who's being asked for Kaye?"

"I'll ask some boys from the Village, there's the Toth Hall contingent. Bela Georgy, Imre Kovacks, Joe Molnar. If there are enough boys, it's a good party, right?"

"Right. What can I do to help?"

"You could help telephone."

"Sure, why not? Hey, wait a sec."

"What's the matter?"

"The first question the kids will ask is, what do we wear? How about a 'Come as you are' party? They wear whatever they've got on when we call them up."

"Connie, you're a laugh a minute. No. I want this to be a real party. Randy's catering and my sisters-in-law will be here to help and I'm going to see if I can round up enough free talent for a combo. Let's make it dressy."

"Meaning what?"

"Just tell everyone it's to be not too casual and let their conscience be their guide."

"Pants are out?"

"No. But nice ones. No blue jeans."

Pete told Kaye about the party the next day, and as Gramp had prophesied, Kaye said, "I don't have anything to wear to a party."

It was a ticklish subject to approach, and Pete had spent half the night tossing over it and then chucked out twenty subtle approaches in favor of the outright honesty that Kaye had said she admired.

"Kaye, I tried to think of a tactful way to approach this and there isn't any that doesn't sound fake. So here goes: In a big family clothes are always being lent and borrowed. We're tall like you, and when we don't want to go out and buy something for a special occasion we pick up the phone and ask each other, 'Hey, what have you got that will do?' "

Kaye was thoughtful. Then she smiled and Pete knew it was going to be all right. "A week ago I would be running down the street, angry and hurt and never wanting to speak to you again. That was a week ago, Pete. Go ahead, pick up the phone."

Pete didn't pick up the phone. She got into the Porsche that evening and drove out to the house where Paul's wife, Joan, now lived alone with two dogs, three cats, four color television sets, two refrigerators crammed full of steaks and sweets, five closets full of clothes, and a big parcel of loneliness. With all that working against her, Pete could never understand how Joan managed to remain a tidy one hundred ten pounds and a size eight.

Joan could be lazy, boring, and self-centered, but she was also generous, with a heart as big as all outdoors. After eating a second supper with her sister-in-law and listening to her oft-repeated sob story about her marriage, Pete shoved back her chair and said, "Joan, a friend of mine who is exactly your size needs a dress for the party we're giving Friday night."

"Well, why didn't you say so two hours ago? Come on, we'll raid the closets."

At ten o'clock Pete pulled away from the split-level ninety-thousand-dollar home in which Paul and Joan had destroyed their marriage, and headed back toward Bamberger Village. On the seat beside her was a large carton which contained three dresses and an assortment of accessories. In the trunk of the car was a lot more: sweaters, skirts, pants, two coats, boots, shoes, blouses, and scarves. She stopped at a public telephone and dialed Kaye's aunt's number.

"Hi, Kaye," she said. "I know it's late, were you in bed?"

"No, watching the late show."

"Would it be all right if I brought over a couple of boxes?"

"Sure, I guess so."

When Pete unloaded the stuff, Kaye protested

at the quantity. Pete reached over and gave Kaye's long hair a playful tug. "Shut up and help me carry the boxes inside. There's plenty more where these came from, Kaye. Happy New Year and have fun deciding what you'll wear Saturday night."

CHAPTER SIXTEEN

Pete listened to the clock in the hall strike eight. Zero hour before a party is worse than zero hour before a game, she thought. On the basketball court you know the hazards. The worst that can happen is that you'll get swamped. But a party! She shrugged. A party was always a dangerous enigma to Pete. The unexpected had a way of happening.

She listened to the sounds in the house. You could tell that it wasn't just any old night in the Phillips homestead. Mary, Dusty, and Mom were puttering about the kitchen, telling the cat to get out of the way. The combo — culled that morning from the ample talent of the Village — was tuning up in the double living room, the old-fashioned parlor of the house and the family sitting room were made one for the evening by the simple expediency of pushing back the sliding doors. The three-piece band had dubbed themselves The Mudflat Pigeons. Pete wasn't sold on the name, but when you were getting a fiddler, a drummer, and a piano man for free, you didn't argue about what they called themselves!

The house was as full of smells as it was of sounds. Spices, apricots, fresh-baked pastry, apple strudel, and *dobos torte,* Mary's famous Hungarian seven-layer cake.

Pete took one last look in the mirror to be

sure the dress she had worn to the Bradford High dance looked as good tonight as it had on that date with Shawn. She felt better in it tonight than she had the first time she had worn it. It was now a familiar friend, something she could forget about while she turned her attention to her guests and having a good time.

As she gave a perfunctory fillip to her wind-blown bangs, she had her mind on something besides her hair. She was thinking of the girl getting ready in the room down the hall. Kaye Brown. Pete had gone down earlier on to pick up Kaye. "You can dress at our house," she had told her on the phone, "and we want you to stay over. It will be a late party, and that way your aunt won't worry." Kaye had come out to the car when Pete called for her, clutching a bat-tered suitcase. Pete had no idea what Kaye had selected to wear. She had never seen Kaye in anything but unpressed slacks and faded sweat-ers that looked four sizes too large. Since Kaye had joined the basketball team she had cleaned herself up, but only someone like Gramp would have seen any latent beauty behind the pallor, the untidy hair, and the poker face.

Pete waited a few moments longer. She could hear people arriving, voices filling the front en-try and the hallway of the old house. "Time to go down," she said aloud to the toy cager that Scott had brought her from the Midwest. From habit, she wound it up and watched it hook a few shots. Then she opened the door and walked quietly down the hall to the guest room. Pete listened. The place was so quiet that she thought maybe Kaye had gone down without her.

She tapped lightly on the door. "Kaye? It's me, Pete."

"Okay, come in."

Pete turned the knob and opened the door. She stopped. For a second she wanted to brush her hands across her eyes to be sure she wasn't seeing a mirage. The girl in front of her was someone she would never have recognized. The Kaye Brown at whom Pete was staring with wide-open eyes was a total stranger.

The dress she had chosen was the one Pete had thought "least likely to succeed" when Joan had tossed it into the pile. "She'll never like that one!" Pete had said to Joan. "It's too plain." But Joan's response had been, "You'd be surprised how well it looks on. It's got style. Of course, it takes a certain type to carry it off."

Now Pete had a long look and she saw what her sister-in-law had meant. The dress was the color of ivory. It was absolutely unadorned, but the fabric was interesting, a textured brocade. The skirt was long and slit, cheong-sam style. This and a tiny mandarin collar gave it an Oriental flavor.

But the wonderful thing was the way it looked on Kaye Brown. It brought out the lines of a trim, lovely figure that had been hidden behind sloppy sweaters and slacks. Kaye had done things to her hair, unbelievable things. She had piled the dark mass in a braided chignon on top of her head and pulled a few tendrils loose around the temples. And she had applied just enough makeup to give color to her pale skin and mouth. The eyes did not need touching up. They were wide with excitement, a deep, deep blue that seemed almost violet.

Never one to mince words, Pete blurted out her reaction. "Kaye, you're a real beauty. Gramp was right. He said you could be!"

"I was hoping you'd think I look all right."

"All right! You're a knockout. Wait till the boys get a squint at you. Come on, let's go down and wow them!"

It was a good party. If there were any hitches, they were so minor that nobody noticed. The Mudflat Pigeons made up in verve and enthusiasm what they lacked in combo experience. They even had a soloist. Angie Alvieri took an evening's vacation from jumping for tip-offs and hurling hook passes to sing with the band. The refreshments were voted the best ever at a home party.

But best of all was what was happening to Kaye.

From the moment she stepped into the large double room, she was the center of attention. Everyone turned and stared.

Pete, standing next to her, put her arm on Kaye's shoulder and said, "Hi, everyone. Let me introduce our guest of honor, Kaye Brown." The girls did a double take, then chattered an overly hearty welcome. But it was their boyfriends who paid Kaye the greatest compliment — that moment of hushed attention which greets the true beauty. It lasted only a few seconds. Then the rush was on. Every boy in the place wanted to dance with Kaye. But the boyfriends soon had to go back to their girls and the stags took over.

Pete, dancing with Shawn, commented. "Kaye's a real stunner tonight, isn't she, Shawn?"

"That she is."

"Gramp saw the possibilities. I've got to hand

it to him. Look at him standing over there in the dining room and gloating." She waved to Gramp and nodded.

Toward the middle of the evening, during refreshments, Kaye sat with Bela Georgy. And after that, he took charge, dancing most of the time with her.

"I've never seen Bela show that much interest in a girl," Pete said to Shawn. "He's usually so quiet and reserved. Who knows, maybe they needed each other."

Around midnight the party broke up, but Pete asked a few special friends, Connie and Bill, Angie and Herb, and Bela, to stay for an "after-party jam session." They turned on the stereo and each couple found their own secluded niche where they could dance and be almost alone. Angie and Herb went out into the hall. Bill steered Connie around the dining room. So Shawn and Pete were left in the big room with Kaye and Bela.

Pete whispered in Shawn's ear, "Could you stand the kitchen and some quiet talk?"

"I can always stand any place where there's food."

"Come on then. Let's leave the two brand-new lovebirds alone. The kitchen's all ours. Mom's in her room and Mary and Dusty have gone home."

Alone in the kitchen, Shawn took Pete in his arms and kissed her. "I thought you intended to go prowling for food," she said, pulling away.

"That I am. But as Gramp O'Hara says, First things first."

"You'd think you belonged to the Phillips family," she told him. "Always quoting Gramp."

With a chicken leg in one hand and a buttered roll in the other, he asked, "What do you want to talk about? You did say we were headed for some quiet talk, right?"

"Right. I want to talk about Burt Johnson."

"Pete, you're too much. Ask one guy to a party so you can discuss his rival."

"You're putting me on. You know very well that I invited you because I wanted to be with you tonight. And the real reason I want to talk to you about Burt is that I honestly happen to need a man's opinion."

"I thought you didn't want to discuss Burt with me. I was all wrong about him and you, you said. Or words to that effect."

"That was then. Things have happened."

"How could they? He's been gone all week."

"He's called me every day. Long distance. Without fail."

"Shows he's thinking of his basketball team."

"Stop joking, Shawn. I'm serious. He didn't have basketball on his mind."

"What did he have?"

"I'm not sure. That's what's bothering me. You know the kind of guy he is."

"Yes, I know the kind of guy he is. What did he say?"

"Not the usual things a man says to a girl he calls up every day. Burt does not have a line. If he did have a line, I could cope with it. It's more what he doesn't say, what he implies, what he lets you read into the pauses and the silences."

"A man of few words, strong actions."

"Anyway, he asked me to save tonight for him and said he'd come home and we'd have a date.

I told him about the party, that we couldn't have a date, but that if he wanted to come, that would be fine. After all, it is a party for the team. I told him to bring a girl if he wanted."

"That was the wrong thing to say."

"So I learned. He was furious. He doesn't fly into a temper and say things he doesn't mean, like you and kids I've known, when he's angry. He gets all cold and silent. Fury under the strength, if you know what I mean."

"I know."

"He told me never to tell him what to do. That he had picked his girl. He said he didn't like flippancy in a woman, even a bright one. I told him if he meant me, I wasn't being flippant, I was being polite."

"I bet that got a quick response."

"Sure did. He said that kind of politeness was for shallow people whose feelings were all on the surface, superficial. Shawn, I'm worried."

"What about?"

"I don't know. It's just a feeling, an intuition of some kind. I promised I'd see him tomorrow. Have a date, the one we didn't have tonight. He said fine, we'd take a ride, have supper, maybe see a movie, ride out to Watch Hill. That's his special spot."

"That old Indian stamping ground, taken over by the Coast Guard?"

"That's right. Shawn, when I see Burt tomorrow, I've got to tell him something that isn't going to be easy. I've been thinking over what Miss Lucia said about dating him. She's right. I stood my ground that day when she and old battle-ax Vaughan gave me a dressing down, but I've thought it over. I'm going to break off with Burt."

"I wouldn't do that, Pete." The words spilled out, fast, impulsively. Shawn meant them.

"I've got to, Shawn."

"Wait until after the basketball tournament, if you must do it. Not now, Pete. You're asking me, Pete, and I'm telling you."

"I can't wait, Shawn."

"Why not?"

She was quiet a moment before answering. She listened to the sounds of the fast-fading party, the stereo, Bill crooning to Connie as they danced in the next room, laughter from the hall as Herb said something humorous to Angie, the soft shuffle of feet on the bare floors.

It had been a great evening. Kaye's evening, really. All that attention. And finding one person she could feel right with. Everything about the party had been a success. It should have left a lovely warm glow inside Pete, the kind of glow you felt when something important turned out right — especially when you had done it _for_ someone else.

She did not feel that glow. She felt concern. The uneasiness you cannot shake off when you know that something in your life isn't quite right.

Shawn repeated his question.

"Why can't you wait **until** after the basketball tournament, Pete?"

"I don't know," she said. "I honestly don't know. But I just feel I have to do it now."

CHAPTER SEVENTEEN

Burt picked Pete up in the latter part of the afternoon.

"Hi," she said as she climbed into the car. "You missed a good party last night. You should have come. How did your week go?"

"I missed you," was his answer. He gave her that long, steady look from which she always had to turn away. "Do you mind if we ride out and talk before we eat?"

"That's great with me. We had a big dinner. Roast beef and all the fixings. Sure, let's ride."

He drove straight out to Watch Hill. Much of the snow had melted and the path up to the observation ridge was cleared, but Burt made no move to get out of the car. He sat a long time, in a brooding silence. Pete was just about to suggest they turn back when Burt said, "I've been thinking about you all week, Pete."

"I've been thinking too, Burt. About us. Burt, I've got something to say and I might as well say it fast. If I don't, I might lose the courage. Like a long hook shot if you wait too long before you let the ball go."

"I'm listening."

"Burt, this is the last time we're going out like this. We mustn't see each other any more. Alone, I mean. At school, of course, we can't help it. But no more dates."

He didn't say anything. He just looked at her.

"Burt, say something. Don't keep staring like that."

"Pete, I've made up my mind. I'm going to marry you."

"Marry me!" Panicking, she opened the door and got out of the car. She stood there, looking at him.

"Yes, marry you. That's why I took this week off, to think. The message came to me loud and clear, Pete. I'm sure about us."

"Don't talk like that."

He got out and came around to where she was standing. He took her in his arms. She pulled back.

"Burt, it's crazy. To think and talk like this. Let me go, Burt."

He held her fast, his voice low-pitched as he spoke to her. "It's not crazy, Pete. It makes a whole lot of sense. We're right for each other. In every way. You love me, don't try to say you don't. A man knows when a woman loves him. And I'm head over heels about you. It started that day a couple of summers ago when I ran into you down in the Village and saw how you had grown up, the kind of woman you had turned out to be, Pete. You're something real, something genuine in a world that is sometimes 90 percent plastic."

"No, Burt. You mustn't talk like this. I won't listen."

"Are you afraid to listen because you'll hear the truth? The truth is what I'm saying. We have everything in common — background, interests, feelings, even dislikes. We have the same approach to life. Head on. We have the same values.

179

A lot of the people who were born and raised in the Village want so much because they have had so little."

"We want a lot out of life too, Burt. Don't kid yourself."

"Sure we do. But not things. Not possessions, not the split-level and the piece of dirt and the house full of junk. We want life itself. *Living*. With meaning and warmth. We want to be involved, helping people, doing things that have meaning. You seem to have been born with that knack. I had to acquire it the hard way. Anyway, we've got it. That zest for total involvement. And we know each other — each other's flaws and weaknesses as well as our good points and strengths. We'll be starting out at a point most couples don't reach for several years. And some couples, never."

"It wouldn't work, Burt."

"Yes, it will. I've got plans for us. I've thought about everything. I'll be teaching in another year. You'll want college. We can arrange it so you'll study near where I teach. I'll be able to help you."

"Paul's promised me my college education, Burt."

"We won't need handouts from your family. It's a mistake to start that way. It binds you. We need freedom — both of us — to be what we are. No dependencies. No obligations."

She put her hands on his shoulders and looked into his face. "Burt, I don't think you listened to me before. I said no more dates. It's ridiculous for us to talk marriage. We aren't going to see each other any more. This is the last time." She paused, and nodded for emphasis. "I mean it, seriously, deeply, finally."

He looked into her eyes and their glances held each other a long moment. Then he turned and walked back to the car. He climbed in. She got in beside him.

After a short silence he asked, "Are you sure, Pete? Are you serious about breaking off for good?"

"I've never been more serious about anything."

"Why?"

"Because I don't see the view from your bridge, Burt. You've got a long-range view. I've got a short one. I'm too young and too green. I don't know anything about getting along with any man outside my family. I've been spoiled by my brothers. In a social situation, on dates, I'm never quite at ease, never comfortable. So how can I possibly think about marriage? Marriage is a full-time job, Burt, and I'm not ready for even part-time employment."

"Doesn't being in love with each other mean anything?"

"It means a lot, but not what you think it does. It means we'd better be careful and watch out for curves in the road. People in love do foolish things. It's wonderful to love another person. It changes everything, the world seems all glowing and beautiful, but it's dangerous too. Burt, believe me, listen to me. Stay away."

He sat a few moments thinking. Then he asked, "Do you mind if I take you right home?"

"No, I don't mind. I think it's a good idea."

Pete was nervous about going down to the

school gym for practice on Monday afternoon. She needn't have been. Burt didn't show. Miss Loudon made a brief announcement telling them that Burt had returned to his college to continue the academic work. He had finished his practice teaching. She was grateful that he had given so generously to the Central High team, and had carried them through the major portion of their tournament season.

The announcement was greeted by a flurry of groans from the girls on the team, groans quickly squelched in deference to Miss Loudon's presence. It was a dull practice. Everyone missed Burt's drive and vigor.

When the girls were alone in the locker room, there was a lot more grumbling. "What's going to happen to us when we play Southport this Friday?" Angie wailed.

"Southport's not our biggest worry," Bretta chimed in.

"Big enough," Tammy argued.

"Sure, big enough," Bretta flared back, "but wait till we play Rockwood on their home ground next week! That's the one where we'll be clobbered."

"Don't talk like that," Connie shouted her way into the rhubarb. "You'll ruin our morale."

Connie walked out with Pete as they left the school and headed for their respective cars.

"What's the story?" Connie asked Pete.

"Translate."

"Do I have to? You had a date with Burt on Sunday. That was yesterday. Today you come in looking as if you've lost your best friend, which you haven't because I am it. So there must have been trouble with Burt. You mooned and sulked through classes, sassed Mrs. Maynard, growled at good-natured Mr. Webb, got a bawling out from Miss Vaughan. What happened between you and Burt?"

"Nothing."

"Don't give me that. A guy doesn't just fade without a good-by. Burt was enthusiastic about our team. He loved his work. The only way it makes sense is that he's out of his skull over you and you had a big hassle. What about?"

Pete managed a grin. "There's Bill over there honking at you. Go tell him to cut out the unnecessary noise before a patrol car rolls in and gives him a summons."

Pete checked in with her mother, saw that Lee was scheduled for supper, said she wasn't hungry and wanted to ride around before she settled down to homework. Her mother asked her if she was feeling all right.

"Great," Pete told her. "Just wound up before the game tomorrow with Clifton. It's one of the big play-off games. And Friday we face Southport. Big week. A touch of court-fright and jitters, that's all."

"I worry when you don't eat properly."

"I'll eat something at the Green Comet."

"Diners! That's no way for a growing girl to eat."

She gave her mother a hug. "This growing gal is all growed, Mom. So don't worry. What's good enough for truck drivers is good enough for anyone!"

"Come back early. Gramp was asking about you. He said you didn't drop in for a breakfast snack and you promised you would."

"I'll call him up when I get back."

"Call him up! Why not run over?"

Pete was already on her way out. She knew why she wasn't going to face Gramp tonight. He would read her mind and feelings clear through. He would keep nagging until she opened up with the whole story about Burt and her.

She drove around a while, down to The Dockside, passed Kaye's house but decided not to go in even before she spotted Bela Georgy's jalopy parked outside. She waited until the Green Comet had eased off on the supper rush, then went on in and found herself a booth at the side. She ordered bacon and eggs, remembered that it was a favorite of Burt's, and wished she hadn't. She was spreading jelly on a piece of toast when she looked up and there stood Shawn.

"Hi, Sherlock Holmes."

"You could invite a guy to sit down."

"Go ahead. It's a free country."

He told the waitress to bring him Boston cream pie and a glass of milk. He watched Pete a few moments before saying, "Connie called me. She said she was worried about you."

"So let her worry. It's a free country."

"The boys' team had a session over scores at Bradford this afternoon. We're ahead in the county and will go on to the state play-offs. I thought you'd want to know, since it was your advice about a bucket shot that brought up the scores."

"I'm glad you're glad."

"You play Clifton tomorrow?"

"Sure. Clifton tomorrow and Southport, Friday night and next week, Rockwood. And to quote the lady with the big mouth on our team, one named Bretta Masi, we are in for a colossal clobbering."

"I heard that Burt has gone back to his school."

"Nothing travels as fast as bad news. Look, Shawn, why don't you drop some change into the jukebox so we won't have to make small talk about big tragedies."

When they went out to their cars, he got in beside her instead of going right over to his.

"Have you talked to anyone about it, Pete?"

"About what?"

"What happened yesterday with you and Burt?"

"Who'd be interested?"

"Connie's worried. Your mother is too. Gramp would certainly be interested."

"I'm not talking."

"Maybe you should. You're too inclined to bottle things up inside you. Spill it. Get it out and you'll feel better."

"You asked for it. Burt wants me to marry him." Shawn didn't answer right away. "How's that for a shock-a-roo?"

"What did you tell him?"

"What I had told him already, that we shouldn't see each other anymore. So he took it literally and did the disappearing act." Shawn kept quiet. "Go ahead, be an I-told-you-so. You warned me to wait until the tournament was over. You should have seen that practice today. It was terrible. If we're that bad tomorrow, Clifton will shellac us."

"Pete, I'm going to say something you may not like to hear, but I'll say it anyway. Your main concern right now shouldn't be whether you're going to win or lose a game of basketball. Your concern should be about the man who asked you to marry him."

"What kind of talk is that? Sure I should be concerned about losing games. Listen, brother, and listen well. If my team loses, then I'm responsible because I did a damnfool thing when I didn't stall Burt until after the tournament. You were right, I should have waited."

Shawn shook his head. "You're wrong, Pete. You're forgetting the most important thing about yourself, that you're a woman. A real woman is a wonderful thing to be. You should be a woman first and a basketball player second. You ought to think about that. If you don't, you could wind up like that mechanical doll you're so fond of. I never liked that doll, Pete. I knew you were attached to it, it being a gift from Scott, but I resented that toy hoopster. It stands for the things that aren't right about you, Pete."

"Like what, for instance?"

"Like I said, you keep forgetting that you're a woman first and a basketball superstar second."

Central High squeaked a victory — such as it was — out of the Clifton game by the narrow margin of two points. Clifton did not have a bevy of great shooters like some of the other teams. Kaye Brown won the game for Central by proving herself to be the number-one rebound artist of the league. Pete began the game in fairly good shape, doing her share of the shooting, but when the pressure was on in the final half, her wrist trouble sneaked up on her. She didn't talk about it. She just hoped it would pass.

It didn't. Friday night they played Southport in the Central High gym. Winter had set in again, there had been some snow earlier in the day and although the crowd that turned out was a good one, it was not the same kind of atmosphere as the night game against Rockwood.

Pete was just as glad that the stands were not so enthusiastic. That kind of pressure got to a player. From the tip-off of the Southport game, she had trouble. Each shot was less accurate. She panicked, and Miss Loudon took her out before she fouled herself out of the game. She finished the final quarter on the substitute bench. Once again Kaye helped to carry Central High through to victory, though Bretta was absent and Connie and Angie were not playing up to par. There was also absenteeism on the Southport team, a factor which helped clinch the victory with the final score: Central High 45, Southport 40.

Pete was so upset after the Southport game that she walked through the next day in a daze. It was Saturday, and she was sure Shawn would show up at the Phillips house in the evening, so she got in the Porsche and rode around.

She stopped and got a newspaper before going into the diner for a hamburger. She read the sports page while she was eating.

"Central High is still in the running for a championship," was the lead sentence, "but what has happened to the girls in green and white? They did not play their usual fast-driving game. Conspicuous by his absence was the assistant coach who has been considered responsible for the fine showing the Central High girls made earlier this season. The report is that

Burt Johnson, on lend-lease from the university where he is preparing to become a physical education teacher, had returned to his academic studies.

"The big question now is: What will happen when Central High faces hard-driving Rockwood next week?"

Pete went back to the car and turned on the radio just in time to snag the tag end of the local news. The voice on the air sounded more doleful than mere words printed on a sheet of paper.

"The girls from Central High defeated Southport in their own gym last evening with a score of 45-40. Southport was handicapped by absenteeism, and Central High didn't make too good a showing, either. Except for the rebounding and the shooting of a newcomer, Kaye Brown, the team lacked the aggressiveness for which it has become noted. Word around town is that the Central High girl hoopsters are in the doldrums because they have lost their young dynamic assistant coach, Burt Johnson. A recruit from teachers' college, Burt went back to take his place behind a desk instead of on the basketball court. More's the pity for Central High with the Rockwood game on the agenda for next week."

Pete switched off the radio and drove on home. Shawn's car was parked in the driveway. He heard the Porsche and came running out of Gramp's cottage, pulling on his jacket.

"Where've you been? You've got the whole family nuts. Your mother is calling up everyone. Tim's in there and so is Paul. Gramp's the only one who kept his cool. I had supper with him, and he kept saying, 'The girl's all right. She's thinking something through. She'll be home.'"

188

"Gramp's the only one who's got any sense." She started to get out but he held her arm.

"Wait a minute. I've got things to say."

"You said a lot already, about me and my mechanical doll. You mean there's more?"

"Why don't you get in touch with Burt? Call him up. Maybe go up and see him if he sounds as if he'd like that."

"I never saw one guy so interested in marrying off a girl friend to another guy."

"I don't mean that. What I'm saying has nothing to do with your marrying Burt. Maybe that would be fine, maybe it wouldn't. It's none of my business. But I do think you're in love with him. I told you that a long time ago. He's serious about you and has paid you the highest compliment a man can pay a woman. Knowing you, Pete, and your downrightness, I imagine your refusal wasn't too gentle. I think you ought to talk to him, to let him know how much he means to you."

"Okay," she said. "I'll think about it."

Sunday, Pete started trying to reach Burt at nine o'clock. The university switchboard gave her a direct line to Burt's dorm. When she called the dorm, she was told that Burt did not answer his signal. No, they hadn't any idea how to reach him. Pete kept trying on and off during the morning and early afternoon. Around three o'clock, the voice that answered said, "Burt Johnson? Wait a minute, I think I saw a note about him." Pete waited anxiously. The voice came on again and said, "Yes, here it is. Burt Johnson. He's gone on a field trip."

"A field trip! Where?"

"It doesn't say. I'm sorry I can't help you. That's all the information we have, here at the dorm anyway."

Pete went back to the Porsche and climbed in. She sat there, running her hands around the steering wheel, thinking. Burt was gone. Off-campus somewhere. Was he staying out of reach on purpose?

CHAPTER EIGHTEEN

When the Central High team ran onto the floor of the Rockwood gym, the stands were already packed with spectators. Pete's team was late. The chartered bus had run into a detour, the driver had made a wrong turn, and they had lost precious time.

A cheer greeted them from the Central High side of the stands. Pete glanced over. Several hundred rooters had come over from Bradford. Bamberger Village was well represented. She spotted her family — Mom, Gramp, Tim, Paul. Lee had turned out tonight too. Scott was missing. He was filming a show for television, in the Deep South.

Pete raised her hand slightly in response to waves from her family. Then she turned to join the queue for warm-up shots. She did quite well during the short practice session. She felt no special problem with her hand. She sank every shot she tried but she found herself thinking, That doesn't mean too much. Let's see what happens when the pressure is on.

While she waited her turn in line for a try at the basket, she sized up Rockwood. Slammer Rose and her sidekick Wicket had evidently patched up their differences. They appeared to be on the best of terms. Pepper Wilcox was being her usual bossy self. Skid Buckley was dribbling all over the court, entertaining the stands with her best imitation of the Globetrotters. There were, however, several noteworthy items which Pete tallied up. Bobbi "the Robot" Walters was nowhere to be seen. Pete scanned the Rockwood bench. No Bobbi. The Rockwood free-throw artist was absent, not in the game. The substitutes in the warm-up line were busy with hard concentration on both their long and their close shots. They were going to be used. One was Sally Butler and the other was Bridie Nolan. Also there was a gangling girl with frighteningly long arms and legs and a young face, all wide eyes and nervous mouth. She looked as if she belonged on a grade school playground, but when she got under that board, she just reached up and shoveled the ball in as if she were doing it with a scoop.

"Who is she?" Pete asked Bretta Masi.

"They moved her from the Rockwood junior varsity. Her name is Tina Harvey. She's a sensational shooter. Look at her slam across the key, skid to a stop, and let that ball go. The way she does it gave her the nickname she's got."

"What is it?"

"Kangaroo."

"That's what she looks like, all right. Seems to me it would be hard defending against that kind of maneuver and shot."

"You can say that again, Pete."

When the PA banged out the lineups, Pete listened to hear who was starting in place of the absent Bobbi Walters. She felt relieved when she heard Bridie Nolan's name instead of Tina Harvey's. The kid was young, a real greener. You could see she was edgy over her first night game. But she was a potential major threat. Pete had hurled too many into the bucket herself not to know championship material when she saw it. In action.

Central High's starting lineup was their old standby. Bretta and Pete as forwards, Camilla and Tammy as guards, and Angie at center. Miss Loudon was keeping Kaye on the bench. Pete tried to figure why. Maybe to let the regulars earn their points for awards. Pete guessed they would send Kaye in as forward when the going got rough. Burt had started something when he had done that back in the previous Rockwood game.

The ball went to Rockwood at the tip-off. They used a fast break right down the middle toward their goal. The passing was superb. Near the keyhole, Central High was able to hold them off on a defensive surge, and the ball zigzagged back and forth between Wicket and Slammer. Slammer got it for the throw at the basket. Pete tried to block the shot, being careful not to hack that quick arm of Slammer's. Slammer pivoted away from the defense and let go a fast one. It banked and settled nicely through the rim.

Rockwood 2, Central High 0.

Tammy, putting the ball in play out-of-bounds behind the end line, threw it to Angie who signaled a playmaker for a quick drive down to the Central High keyhole. Pete got ready to jump for the pass from Bretta. The ball never reached Pete. Skid Buckley intercepted, dribbled down toward the Rockwood end. This time there was no need for that defensive zigzagging between Wicket and Slammer. Slammer got it and heaved. Her aim was sure and her hand steady on the ball. It went in.

Rockwood 4, Central High 0.

It was the beginning of a set pattern of play. Central High would be given the ball out-of-bounds each time Rockwood scored. Pete's team couldn't hold on to it. The Rockwood defense had become a blistering offense. They had learned every way to get the ball from their opponents and they knew how to hang on to it. Sometimes Wicket would smash it into the bucket, but most of the goals were made by Slammer. Pete knew why. Slammer, injured out of the previous game with Central High, had been saving her aggressive hostility for tonight.

Pete was too busy trying to stop Slammer to do much private thinking, but when she did, her thoughts shouted at Miss Loudon, Get Kaye Brown into this game!

It wasn't until the score was 20-4 in favor of Rockwood that Miss Loudon got the message. Pete heard the horn blast for a substitution. She stared over to where Kaye was running to the official's table to report herself into the game.

There goes Bretta, Pete thought. She'll have to go out for Kaye, and it's just as well. Bretta's a good shooter but she's favoring that ankle.

The PA rasped, "Substitution. Kaye Brown going in for Tammy Kovacks."

Tammy Kovacks! Pete thought. Miss Loudon's sending Kaye in as guard! Burt Johnson would never have done that. Sure, Kaye's a defense player, but on this team we need her as forward. It's the psychology of the thing. She can shoot even as a guard, but it's not the same thing. She'll be awfully busy defending and guarding that Rockwood fast break down the middle. As forward, she'd have a free rein at the open target of the basket. Now, she'll have to consider Bretta as part of the shooting sprint. Wow, what a mess!

But Kaye came into that last three minutes of the first quarter and turned the tide. She stopped the fast break down the middle. She got the ball to Pete and Bretta. What Kaye brought into that game was contagious. Pete began to score. When the horn ended the quarter, the score stood 20-14. Rockwood was still ahead, but Kaye had succeeded in blocking Rockwood's fast break and had met their strategy for ball-stealing with a strategy of her own.

During the two-minute intermission, Miss Loudon had the good sense not to burden the girls with her usual pep talk. She let them sit in a circle on the gym floor, catch their breath, and exchange ideas.

There wasn't much talk. The girls looked to Pete to take charge. "Any special plays for the next quarter?" Angie asked.

"Just more of the same," Pete said. "If you and Camilla and Kaye can keep funneling that ball past their strong defense, and Bretta and I can keep our eyes on the target, we'll rack up the goals."

"It's a big if," Bretta said. "My ankle doesn't feel so hot. The game was paced too fast in the first quarter. We won't have anything left for the final pressures."

"Maybe you better let Connie go in for you."

"I'll hold out as long as I can," Bretta said. "Now that we're going good, it would be a shame to miss the fun."

If the first quarter was fast, the second quarter was a wild scramble. It began with a bang. Kaye got the ball from Rockwood and was dribbling down the court getting ready for a pass to Pete when Skid Buckley overshot her mark on a sprint to block Kaye. Kaye, agile and alert, saw Skid coming and sidestepped her, but Skid literally skidded into one of the officials and landed face-down. She came up from the tumble with nothing worse than an abrasion on her left kneecap. But the official and the coaches took her out of the game to be patched up.

Pete watched to see who would come in for Skid. It wasn't Tina Harvey. It was Sally Butler.

She thought, That leaves them with two substitutes on the court and one of their best ball-handlers on the bench. She didn't waste much time trying to figure why the savvy Rockwood coaches had sent in Sally Butler instead of Tina Harvey. She was pretty sure they were saving the recruit from the jayvees for a possible emergency. It was always a gamble with greeners. No matter how good they were at shooting, their debut in a night game could turn into a fiasco. There were too many other factors besides supershooting.

Kaye Brown's defense dominated the first few minutes of that second quarter of the game. Most of the time she would get the ball down to Pete or Bretta, but occasionally she would not be able to complete the pass and would have to shoot for the basket herself. Then she would use that fall-away jumper in which she seemed almost not to be aiming for the basket, but shooting on instinct. Pete would have sworn that Kaye could make a basket with her eyes closed.

Rockwood called time-out when the clock said three minutes to go in the second quarter and the score stood Central High 32, Rockwood 24.

When Rockwood came out of the huddle, both Slammer and Wicket had a new look in their eyes. Pete soon found out why. It was Rockwood's ball. They started their drive for the basket. Kaye was right there directing the defense. This time her fast defensive tactics did not work. Rockwood had a new deal. The name of the game was "screenplay." Or the old "give and go" strategy. Each girl on the Rockwood five was on the job. By a series of continuous passes and screens, they worked the ball down to Slammer, who managed an easy lay-up shot.

Rockwood 26, Central High 32.

With the ball now in Central High's possession. Angie and Kaye brought it down toward the keyhole. Pete waited for the pass. Bretta cut in and was closer. Kaye hefted the ball and there was that second's hesitation. It may have been faking. It may have been one of Kaye's rare moments of indecision. At any rate, the ball went toward Bretta's waiting fingers. It overshot the mark. Bretta leaned backward for the catch, lost her balance, and staggered, to come down hard on her right foot.

Pete dived for the ball and got it. Sally Butler tried to block Pete's shot but Pete made it, a banked shot that ran up another two points for Central High.

As she landed on her feet after the shot, she heard the time-out whistle and watched Bretta leave the court. Miss Loudon sent Connie in.

On the next play, Rockwood again screened for their offensive players. Again the ball went to the Rockwood keyhole. This time Wicket successfully sank it.

Rockwood 28, Central High 34.

Central High's ball, Camilla zooming it to Angie, on to Kaye. This time no hesitation, straight on to Pete. But Pete, blocked by Sally Butler and Bridie Nolan, had to pass off. Connie was in the clear. Pete sent the ball sailing toward Connie's upstretched fingers. Connie caught it, pivoted, and missed her shot. Pete tried for the rebound, caught the ball, and attempted a tip-in. The Rockwood guarding was too close. She missed. The ball rolled on the rim, caromed off, and was instant rebound bait. Five pairs of hands struggled for it.

Bridie Nolan got it, dribbled, then started that "give and go" screenplay toward Slammer at the basket. Kaye's old down-the-middle defense was good, but not good enough for the new screenplay attack. The ball went to Slammer, who sank it just as the horn ended the first half of the game. Rockwood 30—Central High 34.

Pete joined her team as they went down to the locker room for the ten-minute intermission. Meg Mumford, the team's manager, was going the rounds, checking for minor injuries. Tammy had a goose egg. A couple of the girls accepted Band-Aids for scratches or cuts.

"What about you, Pete? How you doing?" Meg asked.

"Okay," she said briefly as she walked away from the crowd gathered around Miss Loudon.

Upstairs she could hear the racket as the spectators milled out into the halls for the intermission. It had been a noisy first half with the stands solidly behind Rockwood. The rooters who had come out to cheer for Central High were far outnumbered by the Rockwood fans filling most of the big gym. So far it had not been a hostile crowd, hostile to Central High that is. Aside from the fact that the Rockwood rooters rose en masse and roared their approval every time Slammer or Wicket sank one, there had not been too much for Pete to cope with. Except for that one small incident. It nagged at her now in retrospect. Every crowd had one — the heckler who sat down near the opponent's basket and ran off at the mouth. Tonight had been no exception. Pete had spotted the guy the second she ran for her first warm-up shot.

"Hey, Phillips, you going to finish on the bench tonight like you did with Southport? Whatsamatta? You miss your private coach?"

She threw off the needling. The guy wasn't concentrating just on her. He had a remark for each of the veteran players on the Central High team. She told herself, No great sweat, he's just letting off steam. There's one at every game.

The pace of that first half had been so stiff that if the clown continued to pass his comments, they were lost in the scramble for the ball —until that last minute of play in the second quarter. It had happened when Bretta reached for the overshot pass and lost her balance and Pete had dived after the ball and got it. As she had raised her arms for the thrust at the basket, she heard the guy's voice cut through that second of hush when the stands are waiting to see if an ace forward will make it.

What he had said was, "You're not going to make it, Phillips. You need your boyfriend out there to help you."

She had made it. A clean shot that had rung up two points for Central High. But for the first time in the game she had felt that slight twist of her wrist, that small turning over as she let the ball go.

She knew all about it. Burt had explained it to her again and again. It was an emotional problem. She had to lick it from inside. It wasn't anything that showed and it wasn't anything that anyone else could help her with. But it bugged her now during intermission as she mentally replayed the first half.

She saw Kaye separate herself from the crowd and move toward her. "Hi, Kaye. Fool thing putting you in as guard."

"Maybe not so dumb. A game isn't all shooting. A lot of games have been won on defensive tactics. Remember, a team has to get the ball and hold it before you can shoot it."

Pete changed the subject. "We've got a heckler."

"Every crowd has one."

"He needled me as I was aiming for that final basket."

"He needled me too. About my father. What's he got against you?"

Pete hesitated, flushed before answering. "Burt Johnson. Called him my boyfriend and said I couldn't shoot without his help. It got to me. I was unsteady on that last shot I made."

"You mean the twisting wrist you told me about?" Pete nodded. "Pete, you've made a lot bigger thing of that than it is. Your last shot was good. You did it. That's all that counts. The important thing is not the way your wrist turns over. The important thing is that your shot was good."

"Just the same I wish you were in the game as forward and we could playmake at the basket."

"Pete, that's another thing I've been wanting to say to you."

"What?"

"This superstar-basketball-ace psychology you've got. You want me up there at the basket so the two of us can go for glory together. Stop playing the one-on-one game, Pete. A basketball has five handles. It's a team thing. It's not the two of us going up for glory in a flare of light. Sure, I can play either offense or defense, but you know something? It doesn't matter which I play so long as the team wins. That's the big thing. Your trouble, Pete, is that you've made basketball your total commitment. My father did that. I saw him fall apart because of it. Don't do it, Pete. Make your commitment to life, and to the people who love you, not to a hunk of inflated leather. When you turn your motivation around, Pete, your wrist will stop twisting."

Pete stood there with her mouth open. The two girls remained facing each other. Pete's heart was beating so fast she could hear it pounding. But she didn't answer Kaye. She just turned on her heel and walked on up to the gym.

When the horn started the second half, Pete knew she was in a different ball game. Kaye Brown's coming in had thrown Rockwood off for the time being. The shock of Kaye's strong defensive combat had helped the Central High forwards to rack up the score. Even the strategic screenplay, the old give-and-go, had not completely stopped Kaye. But now on the first play Pete saw that Rockwood had a new screen. They used the "teaser trap." It was a fake screen. Rockwood began their usual screenplay. Then, instead of playmaking for Slammer to toss the goal, they pretended to screen for her and, presto, Wicket dived for the basket. Completely unguarded, Wicket was able to make a clean shot. Skid, back in the game, had helped with the teaser trap.

Rockwood 32, Central High 34.

The stands were on their feet. The cheerleaders bounced out and led Rockwood in a cheer that rocked the gym. "Make it another! Make it another!" the crowd chanted.

With the ball in Central High's possession, Angie, Kaye, and Camilla were able to bring it down to the keyhole, with the Rockwood defense right on their heels. Connie caught the pass from Kaye, held her hands high as if to attempt a jump shot, was too short to make it over the heads of Bridie Nolan and Sally Butler, and had to pass off to Pete. Pete might have made a tip-in shot except that Slammer was there, blocking. Pete pivoted, dribbled, and prepared for an overhead, her arms high for the release of the ball toward the target. As she was poised for the shot, voices from the front row reached her.

"Miss it, Phillips. You're no hot hand tonight." "Where's your boyfriend, Petie?"

As she let the ball go, she felt her wrist turn over, but the shot was good, a banked shot that did some rolling on the rim and finally plopped in.

Rockwood 32, Central High 36.

Kaye was close to her, maneuvering into play-making position as the ball went into Rockwood's possession.

"Good shot, Pete," Kaye whispered.

"Not so hot. My hand is out of control again. The heckler has brought his gang."

"Don't let it get to you."

"Easier said than done."

Again Rockwood brought the ball down on a fast break and used their teaser trap, but Kaye was ready for Wicket to take the ball for the goal. Again they fooled her, screening for Wicket while Slammer managed an unguarded shot at the basket.

Rockwood 34, Central High 36.

On the next play, Angie lost the ball on a dribble and Rockwood once again took it down to their basket, sinking it for another fast goal, and tied the score at 36-36.

The Rockwood stands went wild.

Central High, in possession, was able to hang on to the ball. Again Angie passed to Kaye who brought it down within easy shooting distance. Pete was momentarily blocked, and Connie took the ball on a throw from Kaye. She dribbled until she found an opening for a pass to Pete, who caught it over the heads of the Rockwood defense. Pivoting to get clear for the shot, Pete whammed into Wicket, who should not have been breathing down Pete's neck anyway. The whistle stopped the action.

The official's arm went up and out in the signal for "time-out — foul." Pete wanted to shout a protest, but she kept her mouth shut. The loudspeaker blared, "Foul on Phillips. Charging." Pete kept her eyes down as the action went to the Rockwood free-throw lane. Wicket toed up for her free shot. Pete, watching the brawny Rockwood forward take a deep breath and bounce the ball, thought her share. It had certainly not been a clear-cut case of charging. It could have been called overguarding or a double foul. But you couldn't argue with officials on another team's home court.

The free-throw shot was good. Rockwood 37, Central High 36.

With Central High again in possession, Pete had another foul called on her. This time she had collided with Slammer. The thought struck her: They could be deliberately trying to foul me out! Again the free throw was good. Rockwood 38, Central High 36.

Pete was extra careful on the next play. She fell back for her shot, into the midcourt, and made it a hook shot. Despite the heckling voices shouting, "Miss it, Phillips, your boyfriend's not here to see it!" she sank the shot, tying the score once again at 38-38. The boos from the Rockwood side were deafening.

Here it comes, Pete thought. The pressure is on.

For the next five minutes, the game was two-on-a-seesaw. First Rockwood would take possession and make a goal. Then Central High would make the drive to their basket and sink a shot. The score zoomed to 48-48. Pete once again had a foul called on her when, dodging the Rockwood zone defense, Bridie Nolan closed in on her, overguarding it seemed to Pete, but Pete got the blame for pushing.

As the PA announced, "Foul on Phillips, push-ing," Pete heard the horn and saw Joan Redford, one of Central High's substitutes at the scorer's table. The PA told the story. "Redford going in for Phillips." It was small consolation that Bri-die Nolan missed her foul shot.

Kaye gave Pete the "Don't let it throw you" signal as Pete walked off the court. She slumped down on the bench and Meg Mumford brought her a towel. While she mopped up, Meg whis-pered, "You're being saved for the last quarter."

"What's left of me," Pete muttered.

She watched the last two minutes of the third quarter with moist hands and a galling taste in her mouth. The other day she had fouled and fouled badly, but tonight it had not been a clear-cut case. If there had been a photo finish of those three "fouls" of mine, Pete thought, they would have seen that, in each case, the guard's arms came up at the horizontal position that split second before contact. That means they were at fault. Smart strategy, she thought, and it worked. It got me out of the game during the critical end of the third quarter.

The quarter ended with Rockwood ahead 54-48.

During the two-minute intermission the Cen-tral High girls lay face down at the floor. It was a tired team. Kaye was most tired of all. Miss Loudon was fussing over her. "You'd better rest at the start of the quarter." When the horn called them back, Pete looked over at Miss Lou-don. The coach made no signal for her to return to the court. Joan was still in for Pete, and Tammy was sent in for Kaye. Pete leaned forward and watched the quarter begin. There was something special to watch. Tina Harvey was in the game for Wicket.

It was a bad scene for Central High. The greener from Rockwood was sensational. She could shoot from any spot on the floor. In the first three minutes of play, Rockwood racked up five goals. Miss Loudon kept her glance averted. Pete wanted to shout, If you're going to put Kaye and me in, it better be now! At last Miss Loudon motioned to them. They ran over to the scorer's table and reported in. Joan and Tammy came out.

A chorus of boos followed them across the court. Pete listened to the cheers for Rockwood, the noisemakers, the rolling murmur of voices and the shouts, "Hold them, Rockwood. Keep shooting!" As Pete passed Kaye, she whispered, "Block the new kid, the greener, and I'll do the rest." Pete watched the ball come toward her. It was a strange feeling. A lonely feeling. She stood waiting for the pass. She got the ball and aimed, a hard one right on target.

Rockwood 64, Central High 50.

Pete didn't look at the scoreboard. She knew she must not. If she thought about the score at a time like this, she would handicap herself. There was only one thing to think about. Shooting. Getting that ball and dropping it into the basket as fast and often as she could. She signaled Kaye for total action. The big drive that would bring the ball down to her as fast as possible.

Kaye would know how. She would know how to keep the ball from Rockwood and get it down to Pete. In the next minutes Pete had racked up five goals. On the last one, Bridie fouled her in the act of shooting. Her free throw was good.

Rockwood 64, Central High 61.

The horn warned that there were two minutes left in the game. The stands were bedlam. The tension on the court was so strong she could feel and taste and smell it. Rockwood was going to try to beat the clock. That was for sure.

With Rockwood in possession, it was clear that Skid would try to out-dribble the clock. She did try but lost the ball to Angie. Boos, catcalls. It was Central High's ball. Kaye signaled to Pete to call time-out. In the huddle, Pete leaned forward, her hands on her hips. She was breathing hard.

"Two more goals and we make it, Pete," Kaye told her.

"My hand is losing control. On the last shot, I almost missed. Kaye, I'm not sure I can stick it out."

"You haven't any choice, Pete. It's not *can* you stick it out. You *have* to stick it out."

They went back into the game.

The Rockwood rooters were standing up, screaming for victory. The gym was a madhouse. Pandemonium on wheels. Two goals to go. And only two minutes left, while Rockwood would fight to get possession. If they did, that was the finish. They'd try to beat the clock.

Pete watched the ball zoom toward her upstretched fingers. The Big D from Rockwood buzzed around her like flies. One thing she mustn't do was to foul. Dribbling, she faded back to midcourt. As she hefted the ball for a shot, she heard the roar from the stands. She heard the heckling too. "Miss it, Phillips. Miss it!" She smelled the sweat and the rubber. She felt the tremor in her hand.

The shouts from the stands faded. She shut out everything but Kaye's voice. *It's not can you stick it out. You have to stick it out.*

She let it sail and she knew it was good.

Rockwood 64, Central High 63.

The roar from the stands was deafening as Rockwood got possession. The clock said one minute to go. Slammer took it out for her team. Slammer was in charge. Pete guessed their strategy.

Slammer would pass to Skid. Skid would dribble away the last minute of play. Out of nervousness Slammer fumbled the pass. The ball missed its target and bounced past Skid's surprised face. The scramble that followed was classic. Ten pairs of hands and legs went after the ball. Heads bumped heads. Bodies collided. For one wild second Pete thought she had her hand on the ball. She lost it. It went to the greener on the Rockwood team. Tina Harvey clutched the ball to her, then started dribbling.

For a split second Pete thought she was seeing things in a dream. *Tina Harvey was dribbling toward the Central High basket!*

The kid's confused, Pete thought. That huddle did it to her. Pete ran hard toward her own basket.

Tina realized her mistake, braked to a stop, and started dribbling back. Pete was beside her. Pete reached out and slapped the ball out of Tina's control. Dribbling away from the confused greener, Pete took the ball closer to the Central High basket.

She heard the stands starting the chant that indicated the last ten seconds of play. "Ten — nine — eight . . ."

She spotted Kaye, near the keyhole, waiting for a rebound in case Pete's shot missed. Pete didn't have time to think it through. She had to act, and act fast. As she let the ball go to Kaye her thoughts raced along with it. I owe that girl, she thought. *I owe her!*

Kaye caught the ball easily.

"Six — five — four . . ." the stands chanted.

Kaye raised the ball high in her right hand. It was almost as if she wasn't looking at the basket. It was as though she knew exactly where it was without looking. She let the ball sail. It hit the backboard with a resounding whack as it struck the exact spot where Kaye had aimed. Pete watched the ball plunk through the rim.

The scoreboard flashed: Rockwood 64, Visitors 65, as the horn sounded.

CHAPTER NINETEEN

It was April but it was warm enough to have the windows of the old cafeteria of Central High wide open on this special evening of the spring sports banquet. Most of the speeches were over. Traditionally, the boys' awards were given out first, and then the girls on the team received their letters. Pete stared down at her empty dessert plate. The zero hour was moving in on her. This was the moment to which she had been looking forward with mixed feelings. Pleasure and dread. Dread, because she felt a quiet terror every time she had to make a speech. Pleasure, because it was a speech she really wanted to make.

Mr. Irving, supervisor of physical education for the city, was acting as master of ceremonies. He shuffled the sheaf of papers in his hand. There was an undercurrent of excitement in the cafeteria over the forthcoming announcement, the last of the evening. It was to be the announcement of the girl for the Most Valuable Player award. Mr. Irving rapped for attention. He waited for the murmur of voices to fade into silence.

"My friends," he began, "it is now my privilege to introduce as the next speaker a girl whom I am obliged to call unique in the annals of local sportsmanship.

"The other day I called Pete Phillips to my

office. I wanted to tell her that she had been voted the Most Valuable Player of our league. I naturally expected Pete to jump with joy as any girl would under the circumstances. She did not. Instead, she quietly thanked me and said that, rather than accept the award, she would like to ask a special favor of me.

"Because that favor was so unusual, I am going to let Pete Phillips tell you about it herself." He turned toward Pete, smiling. "Pete, it's all yours."

She got up. Her knees were rubbery and her palms were as moist as if she were standing in Madison Square Garden and getting ready to throw a hook shot. She swallowed the lump in her throat and began in a husky voice.

"It wasn't that I didn't want the award. I'm not that bighearted and anyone who knows me well, as a lot of you do, will agree." She waited for the slight wave of laughter to pass. "It's just that I felt someone else in this room deserves it more."

There was a flurry of interest, and she waited for the kids to settle down before she went on.

"Before I tell you who the girl is, I want to ask you to go back with me to the final quarter of the Rockwood game, to the final few minutes, in fact. Most of you either played in that game or sat up in the Rockwood stands and watched. You know that certain factors made it necessary for yours truly to carry the brunt of the shooting throughout the first three quarters, when the odds were stacked against Central High.

"The last two minutes of play were more than I thought I could take. I was dog-tired. We had a hostile Rockwood crowd down front heckling us. And let me say right here that, throughout this season, I had been fighting a personal battle with myself on the basketball court.

"Those final few moments of that game, I could think of only one thing, either running off that court or going ball shy — letting someone else try for the baskets. I was afraid to shoot, afraid I wouldn't be able to control my shots. Central High took a time-out. In the huddle, I turned to the girl whom we are about to honor and I told her I was worn out. I didn't have anything left. 'I'm not sure I can stick it out,' I said.

"This girl looked me straight in the eye. She didn't mince words. She laid it right on the line. I'll never forget what she said to me in that huddle. She snapped out, 'Pete, it's not *can* you stick it out. You *have* to stick it out.'

"Just those six words. You *have* to stick it out. You know why that got to me? Because it was a language I understood. The language of Bamberger Village where so many of us were born and raised.

"The team went out of that huddle and back into the Rockwood game and won it — together. The girl I want to honor made the winning shot — after sparking the whole team with her confidence and drive.

"So I'd like to ask that girl to step forward. Will Kaye Brown please come up here?" Kaye got up slowly. Pete watched her push back her chair and look around, puzzled. Connie Anderson had to give her a slight nudge before she moved toward the front of the room.

Pete reached over to where the trophy rested

on the speaker's table and held it out. "Kaye, it is my heartfelt pleasure to give you the Most Valuable Player award for your contribution to basketball sportsmanship."

Pete watched Kaye's eyes as her trembling hands got a firm grip on the trophy. The eyes were shining with something fresh and bright and wonderful, a new lease on life. . . .

It was late when Pete turned the Porsche into Bamberger Village and headed for home. She had said good night to Shawn at Connie's house. They had all parked their cars there earlier and piled into Bill's station wagon to ride out to Bruno's Pizzeria, the traditional place for Central High teams to go for pizzas, Cokes, and a dance or two after an Awards Banquet.

As Pete turned down the street, she saw the Phillips house well lighted, so she guessed that Mom, and perhaps Gramp, was waiting up for her. But before she reached the drive, she spotted something else. It was a car she recognized, parked close to the curb in front of the house. Burt was standing beside it.

She pulled in behind the car and got out.

"Hi, Burt," she said. "Long time no see."

"I've been waiting for you."

"You been waiting here long?"

"Half an hour. I knew you'd be at the sports banquet and Bruno's Pizzeria afterward and about when you'd be home."

"It's warm for April, isn't it?" she said, feeling silly, because there were so many things she wanted to say to Burt and couldn't say any of them.

"Want to take a ride?"

"The family's waiting up, I guess I shouldn't."

"I've been in to see them. It's all right. I told them we wouldn't be late."

Watch Hill looked different with the snow gone and spring balminess in the air. They climbed up the incline to the ridge and stood looking down on the moonlit water. They stood close, Burt's arm snuggling her to him.

"I didn't want to leave the team, Pete. I didn't want to run out on you, either."

"I knew that. I knew it was something you had to do. There are times in life when a guy stays and takes it and times when a guy doesn't."

"Then you didn't blame me."

"More likely I blamed myself."

"What for?"

"For not facing up to being a woman first and a basketball player afterward. Shawn put me wise to that. Kaye talked about it too, in her own way. She said it was total commitment to the wrong thing. She ought to know. She had a father who made the same mistake."

"That was a fine thing you did for Kaye," he said, brushing Pete's hair back from her cheek. "Gramp told me about it — giving her the Most Valuable Player award."

"She deserved it." They were quiet for a while. Then Pete said, "I'm going to ask you a question, Burt, but before I do, I want to tell you something."

"Go ahead."

"It's something that happened a long time ago, when I was a kid, around ten or so. The rest of the girls — Connie, Angie, Tammy, Camilla,

214

the crowd of kids I grew up with — were all beginning to pick boyfriends for themselves, even starting to 'go steady' in an infantile sort of way, if you know what I mean, a movie matinee with a special boy, soda pop afterward, funny little gifts, and that kind of thing, the boy gives you his favorite sweater and swipes your bandanna. You know."

"Yes, I know. I grew up in Bamberger Village too."

"Well, this day, my brothers were in one of their teasing moods. Terrible. They could be hellions that way when they wanted to, and I was the only sister to tease, so I would get it full blast. This day, they got to harping on boyfriends and why all the girls in the Village that were my friends had a special boy or two or three and I didn't have anyone yet. They were merciless — said I'd be an old maid, said I didn't know how to interest a boy, that I was trying too hard to compete with them. And I guess I was."

"An only girl and seven brothers, what did they expect?"

"Gramp was there, taking it in, every word of it. He stood it as long as he could, then he shoved his way into the argument. I remember his exact words as if it were yesterday. 'I'd like to take part in this donnybrook,' he said. 'Now, my fine young grandsons, you listen to me and listen well. What you say about your sister, Pete, may be true in part. She's self-reliant and independent and she competes with you boys, that she does. But I'll be telling you for a fact that your sister has the makings of a fine woman and one thing is sure, she will know a real man when she sees one. The day will come when she'll be finding that real man and she'll be picking him out herself. This, my fine grandsons, is a far better thing for a woman to do than to sit around the house and sew doilies and wait for some namby-pamby ladies' man to come running after her. Pete will pick her own man in her own time, that she will.' "

She turned toward Burt and reaching up took his face between her hands. "I said that after I told you the story I wanted to ask you a question, Burt."

"I'm listening."

"I've found my 'real man,' Burt. What I'm asking you is, will you marry me?" She rushed on, afraid he might answer before she said everything she wanted to say. "I don't mean right away, not this year and maybe even not next year. But who can say for next year? What I'm trying to tell you is that I've had time to think, and what's more important to feel, to know the real feelings inside me — about you, about us. Sometime, when we're both ready for it, I hope you'll marry me, Burt."

He took her in his arms and held her close and kissed her. Snuggling her head against his jacket, he asked, "Pete, what made you change your mind?"

"I don't know for sure, a lot of things, I guess. When you went away, nothing seemed the same, nothing seemed right anymore. Even on a great day, the air seemed polluted, and my food tasted like straw, and the birds were singing off-key, and the sky was upside down, and people seemed to be walking around on their heads. And I couldn't think straight, I just couldn't think right at all. And I felt this terrible closed-in feeling, like I was locked in, locked into myself. And then I saw something I had not realized before."

"What was that, Pete?"

"I used to think that love was a kind of bondage. I saw that this just wasn't so. Real love brings freedom, Burt, freedom from self. We cannot really love until we break out of the shell we call 'myself' and reach out to the other guy. And then it dawned on me, that the important things that have been done for this world, and all the good things one person has ever done for another, must have been because of this kind of love."

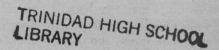
TRINIDAD HIGH SCHOOL
LIBRARY

TRINIDAD HIGH SCHOOL
LIBRARY